NAILED

TO THE

WALL

JAYNE RYLON

eBook ISBN: 978-1-941785-32-4
Print ISBN: 978-1-941785-61-4

Ebook Cover Art By Angela Waters
Print Book Cover Art By Jayne Rylon
Interior Print Book Design By Jayne Rylon

OTHER BOOKS BY JAYNE RYLON

Touch of Amber
Long Time Coming

COMPASS BROTHERS
Northern Exposure
Southern Comfort
Eastern Ambitions
Western Ties

COMPASS GIRLS
Winter's Thaw
Hope Springs
Summer Fling
Falling Softly

PLAY DOCTOR
Dream Machine
Healing Touch

STANDALONES
4-Ever Theirs
Nice & Naughty
Where There's Smoke
Report For Booty

RACING FOR LOVE
Driven
Shifting Gears

RED LIGHT
Through My Window
Star

DEDICATION

For Eleanor Lees, the undisputed queen of *that's what he/she said* jokes. I especially love it when you do it to yourself (that's what she said!). You crack me up.

CHAPTER ONE

"**M**y hands are full, stick it in my mouth." Devon wrapped her lips around the stem of the lavender rose Kate wagged in her direction.

Kayla sing-songed, "That's what *he* said."

Devon choked. She met her friend's gaze in the mirror, then burst out laughing. It was even funnier because her joke held a kernel of truth. When their husbands and the rest of the crew got together for one of their steamy sessions, the logistics of five guys going at it made for some interesting challenges.

Somehow she managed not to drop the pretty prop clasped between her teeth. The laces on the corset Morgan had been tightening around Devon's slim ribcage slipped in the aftermath of their raucous exhalations.

"Shit, sorry," she mumbled around the flower, hoping it had no thorns. Then she forced herself to calm down. An extended sigh deflated her torso. She yanked taut the panels of the garment she attempted to squeeze into, less certain than ever about this foray into femininity.

Being girly was not her strength.

Morgan seized the opportunity to cinch the black satin. Embedded with boning, it hugged Devon tight. A few flicks of Morgan's fingers left the long tails of a bow dancing over the swells of Devon's ass. She'd seen postage stamps bigger than the matching thong they'd bought to complete her ensemble. It didn't protect the skin bared between her skimpy undies and the top of her fishnets from the brush of the soft laces.

"Damn, you're smoking hot." Morgan surveyed her handiwork before nodding.

Devon angled her torso sideways to the mirror, cupped her breasts, then plucked the rose out of her mouth. "It's magic. It makes even me look stacked."

"Because it squishes your already tiny waist down to the size of my pinky." Kayla pouted. "I hate you."

Ever the practical one, Kate marched over. She slipped her hand around the edge of the bustier. "Are you sure you can breathe okay? How does it feel?"

Devon twisted from side to side, testing the bounds of her hindered flexibility. "A little uncomfortable, but nothing I can't handle.

Sort of a nice pressure once you get used to it."

"That's what *he* said," Morgan chimed in this time.

Another round of giggles bled some of the nervousness from the gathering of scantily clad girlfriends who milled about in Kate's living-room-turned-studio.

Relief relaxed Devon enough that she blurted, "Okay, so, don't laugh. I know we've seen each other naked more often than with clothes on. We've gone wild and crazy during not one but *three* bachelorette parties scandalous enough to require a Vegas-esque pact of silence. And I can't count the number of nights we've spent watching each other or our guys get fucked senseless. But suddenly this seems a little... I don't know."

"Intimate?" Kate supplied.

"Yeah." Devon gnawed her lip. Sometimes it sucked being the youngest, least experienced, of the bunch. She was the newest too, though it'd been almost a year since they'd adopted her as the runt of their tightknit group. Their family-by-choice was comprised of a five-man construction crew and their four female lovers. "Am I the only one who's sweating?"

"No." Morgan plopped onto the padded bench Mike had painstakingly restored for

Kate, who had fallen in love with the previously half-rotted carcass at a garage sale. Devon smiled, recalling how they'd struggled to jam the thing in Kate's tiny hybrid sedan. In the end, she'd had to ride to Kate and Mike's place on Kayla's lap while their treasure occupied the other half of the backseat. They'd laughed the whole way.

The furniture fit in the renovated house Kate had inherited as if it had been designed specifically for the nook by the stairs. Devon considered her niche in the crew and could relate.

Morgan's sudden drop to the tufted-fabric seat fluffed out the frilly edges of the microskirt on her naughty peek-a-boo nighty. She wafted cool air across her artfully painted face with a vintage hand fan. Sultry and sleek, she could have come straight out of a girly magazine or maybe the classiest of Amsterdam's famous red-lit windows.

"Let's jump right in and do this." Devon rolled her eyes when Kate opened her mouth to interject. "I know. That's what *he* said. Seriously though, if we don't get a move on, we'll be more nervous than a roofer in an electrical storm. Next thing we know, Kate will have chewed a hole in her lip and my hair will wilt like week-old lettuce. I can't believe you were able to fluff it so damn high to begin with. Anyway, that's not going to be a good look for our boudoir photos. Our pictures will suck and our husbands will leave us and we'll all die old and lonely."

"If they're hideous, we'll figure something else out," Kate shushed her.

"We're running out of time to come up with an alternate Valentine's Day present." Devon paced. "It has to be perfect for them."

"Stop before you hyperventilate, munchkin. This only feels weird because we let our guys maintain their illusion of control." Kayla hugged Devon. Warmth seeped into her from her friend's embrace. It settled her like a shot of steamed milk before bed or the afterglow of a really good orgasm. "With them gone, things are out of sorts. I miss them too, you know."

"Stupid ice-fishing trip." A lonely long weekend hadn't sounded so awful when the guys had first proposed it. The sparkle in their eyes at the thought of three whole days filled with beer, trash talk and freezing their nuts off had guaranteed that none of the women objected. "Why couldn't Joe's Uncle Tom have brought his gang to Kayla's resort instead of luring our crew to the middle of nowhere? What if they get attacked by a herd of psychotic moose? Or sucked into a vat of maple syrup? Neil has a massive sweet tooth.

I could see him leaning over for a taste and tumbling right in."

"Um." Kay looked like she'd bitten into a lemon. "All those crazy cousins are more than my retreat can handle. They're so feral they make our husbands look tame by comparison. No thanks. Canada is barely far enough away. It's only one more night. We'll survive. And so will the crew. I'm pretty sure."

Devon sighed. "Do you know how many spooky noises our pipes make at two o'clock in the morning? I've never noticed that before. It got so bad last night I stayed up until dawn trying to fix some of the loose joints in our ductwork. Granted, HVAC isn't my specialty. That's more of Joe's thing. But I swear, I'm usually pretty terrific with my hands. Not today. I sucked big time."

"That's what *he* said." Kayla winked.

Devon smacked her forehead with the heel of her hand.

"There aren't any monsters under your bed or in your freaking H-whatever. You've just never listened hard enough before. Probably because you're moaning too loud to hear the creaks and pops or knocked unconscious by a zillion big Os in a row." Morgan wiggled her eyebrows.

"Good point. But that's not my fault. You know how it goes. Everyone has to have a turn. And then sometimes I have seconds. Or fifths. Or seventeeths. I mean, sex with James *and* Neil is the best-tasting, calorie-free dessert of all time." Devon pouted. Spoiled? For sure. She liked it that way. "How can I resist the temptation of *two* fine men in my bed? And once I'm snuggled between them, the rest of the world melts away."

"They make it easy to surrender. All of our guys do. They have a knack for affection—giving and getting. It's part of who they are. Maybe it's time to sprinkle a little girl power in the mix." Kate's lips angled up in a wry smile. She propped her hand on her hip. Manicured fingers splayed over the delicate ivory lace of her cat suit. Skintight and translucent, it covered every inch of her yet left nothing to the imagination.

A pair of nude platform heels added to her stature. They made her legs seem longer than the fifteen-foot extension ladder the crew used for painting exteriors. The wife of the crew's foreman could have doubled for a pinup girl given the lustrous fall of her loose, wide curls.

"What did you have in mind?" Kayla slung her arm over Kate's shoulder and bumped her hip into their friend's. The flattering lines of Kay's ruched, purple merrywidow complimented the troublemaker glint in her eye and the assortment of body art escaping the limited cover-up provided by her lingerie. Wicked black leather boots rose above her knees, completing her alternative ensemble.

"Well, let's see how sexy we can make these pictures, shall we?" Kate winked. "I figure it won't take much to have the crew eating out of our hands. They'll be our extra-horny hostages. Then maybe we can draw up a list of our demands."

"Sounds like a plan to me." Devon stalked to the tripod standing in the center of Kate's living room, which they'd cleared of furniture other than a cameo-backed occasional chair and mounds of cushions they intended to use as props. They'd also strategically crumpled a creamy silk sheet before hanging it as their backdrop.

She aimed the digital SLR camera at the top of the mountain of pillows they'd arranged earlier. While she fiddled with the focus, her best friends entered the frame one by one. Lots of natural light from the late-afternoon sunshine flooded the space, making the women practically glow. Or maybe their flushes were a side-effect of envisioning what would happen when their guys got a hold of the final product of today's session.

The photography classes Devon had taken at the local community college would pay off a thousand times over.

"Okay, I have the settings where I want them. But if we'd like to review the images as we take them with the remote, we'll have to rely on my laptop. I tried to connect it before. The video cable wouldn't work although I swear it's the right one. I'll give it another shot. If that doesn't do the trick, we'll have to wing it. Where's Dave and his geeky tendencies when you need them?"

Before she'd finished mumbling, her friends began shouting out suggestions in the tried-and-true fashion of onlookers providing impromptu tech support. Devon ignored them. She fiddled with the connections while the bombshell peanut gallery peppered her with advice.

"Nothing's happening. Push the wire in deeper. Make sure the connection is tight." Morgan surrendered a mini-snicker.

"Maybe you're aiming for the wrong hole?" Kate asked with faux innocence.

"Take it out, then put it back in again." Kayla joined the fray. "Give it a tug and wiggle."

"Damn it. Let me concentrate." Devon bit her lip to avoid granting them satisfaction by cracking up. Had they forgotten she was supposed to be the juvenile one of the bunch?

She focused on the stubborn cable. The slightly misshapen prong looked like it might have been stepped on. Probably by someone wearing steel-toed construction boots if she had to guess. Crap, this had to work or they would be shooting blind. No way would they be able to arrange a second session without their guys getting suspicious.

She changed the angle of her laptop for better access, then shoved hard enough to void her warranty.

"Good idea. Sometimes it's easier to slide it in from the rear." Morgan hid her smile behind her hand.

The cable locked into place.

"I knew I could work it in if I was patient. Or barring that, if I rammed it in. Whatever works to open that bitch up." Devon laughed as deeply as she could, given the snug fit of her corset. "All right already, I surrender. That's what *he* said."

The other three women clapped. Morgan chortled until she snorted. Of course that set off another round of giggles. By the time they'd recovered, their cheeks were flushed and their eyes were bright.

Devon hustled to join the gathering. She tipped onto her side in the foreground, propping her cheek on one hand. With the other buried beneath a silk pillow, she depressed the remote shutter release. Several frames were captured in rapid succession.

Oohs and *aahs* rained around her as the women caught sight of themselves on the laptop screen. Their reactions led to some unusable shots dotted with awkward expressions.

They took the visual feedback and adjusted their poses, displaying themselves to the best advantage in their naughty lingerie. Kate leaned over the chair-back, thrusting her pert ass into the air. Morgan and Kayla stood back to back. Each bent one leg to display their shapely thighs. Devon tipped onto her tummy for a few cheeky shots, her stilettos kicking in the air as she touched one fingertip to her pursed lips. Then she curled up at the other women's feet, shifting the splay of her legs until she threatened to expose herself to her friends, their lovers and anyone else who went digging around on her memory card.

"Yeah, I think they'd like some raunchier ones too." Kate switched her stare to each of them in turn. "Don't you?"

"Yes." Kayla knelt on the cushion Devon had used to prop herself up. "Come here."

Devon obeyed automatically.

Kay wrapped her hand around Devon's nape, squeezed gently, then guided her close. Close enough to kiss if she'd wanted to. Instead, she paused a hairsbreadth away and let the camera immortalize the moment of anticipation.

Sweet strawberry lip gloss tempted Devon's tongue to peek out and steal a taste from Kayla's mouth. She held the urge in check. It wouldn't be the first time they'd kissed. But it didn't feel right to indulge without Neil, James and Dave there to enjoy the moment.

From what she could see of the next few shots—a couple of which involved Kate spanking Devon playfully while the others cheered her on—the guys would cherish their gift almost as much as they did their new wives.

In her case, their committed life partner.

Devon let her smirk linger for a few more frames before tipping forward and eliminating the chasm between her and Kayla. Too bad Morgan's excited cry startled them apart a few instants later.

"That's the one, right there." She did a little fist pump. "It's perfect. We all looked hot. I think that's a wrap. Agree?"

"Yeah, this thing is starting to itch and there's no Mike waiting upstairs to rip it off me." Kate frowned.

Devon didn't meet Kayla's gaze as she popped to her feet, practically racing to the camera and laptop stations. She disconnected the equipment, packing each component into a neat bundle before dropping it into her carrying case.

When she pivoted, she realized the other three ladies had wandered off to change and gather their belongings. Kayla returned just as Devon tucked the last of the supplies away.

"Dev—"

"I'd better try to wrestle this corset off before it gets too late. You know I'm not a fan of driving in the dark." Truth was, the frisson zipping up her spine had more to do with the questions in Kayla's gaze than her nightmares of hitting a deer or breaking down in an unfamiliar neighborhood.

Damn her guys for leaving her alone for three whole days. Her system had grown accustomed to regular relief. The lack of orgasms must have been turning her brain to mush and making her senses go haywire, as though she were in endorphin withdrawal. Hell, she probably was.

As Devon prepared to make her escape, a hand landed lightly on her forearm. She glanced over her shoulder. Directly into Kayla's eyes.

"If you'd rather not be alone, you're welcome to stay at my place tonight." She smiled with enough warmth to soothe the goose bumps rising on Devon's skin. "You're *always* welcome."

A reflexive refusal hovered on the tip of her tongue.

Kayla's fingers trembled where they touched.

Devon reconsidered in a flash. It hadn't been an easy offer. They had too much at stake to fuck things up. Who was she to reject Kayla? Especially when Dev wanted to accept the invitation more than she craved the pink leather tool belt she'd spotted at Chicks Construct?

"Thank you." She smiled. "It's been a long time since I had a slumber party."

"Oh, damn. That's a great idea. Why didn't we think of it before?" Morgan rejoined them, Kate trailing a handful of steps behind. "We could rent a bunch of movies, do each other's hair, whip up a batch of skinny margaritas, compare notes on our guys..."

"This might be a private party." Kate tried to rein Morgan in.

Kayla looked to her three friends. She shrugged at Devon.

"Since when is anything between us a secret?" Devon grinned. "The more the merrier and all that jazz."

"Yes! I think we should watch *Dirty Dancing* first." Morgan started a list while Kate ran upstairs to pack an overnight bag. "Then *Breakfast Club*, and maybe a slasher flick."

"No, no." Devon shook her head vigorously. "I don't do scary shit."

"Don't worry, we'll be there to protect you." Kayla smiled.

"God only knows what kind of Bigfoot lives in your woods, or maybe a creepy lake monster. No point in tempting fate." Devon crossed her arms over her chest.

"I think it might be too late for that." Kayla met her stare. Then she grabbed for one of Devon's bags and slung it crossbody. "Almost ready?"

"I think so. Let me change first." A wicked grin escaped before she could think better of it. "Unless you'd like me to ride naked to your house. No sense in putting clothes on only to take them off again when we get there."

"Just because it's a naturist retreat doesn't mean you have to…"

"I know. But I've kind of gotten used to it." Devon shrugged. "It is pretty cold out today, though. I think I should at least wear my overcoat."

Kayla choked as Devon sauntered off, adding an extra swing to her step. She wished her men had been there to witness the exchange and maybe give her the push she needed to see what could evolve if they let it.

CHAPTER TWO

Devon popped another handful of caramel corn into her mouth, despite the fact that the credits of their third movie scrolled past on the muted TV. She smiled as she thought back to Dave and Kayla's first fight—a battle over the installment of the enormous flatscreen. Secretly, she was glad her friend had compromised and allowed the technology in her haven. The custom oak cabinet the crew had devised to hide any trace of ugly black plastic was a work of art.

Crispy, coated kernels surrendered to her chomping. She licked sticky sweetness from her fingers. When she looked up, she caught Kayla peeking at her from the corner of her eye.

Devon knocked her knee into her friend's. "Want some of this?"

"Yeah." Kayla made no move to grab a snack.

Morgan refilled their pretty, hand-blown margarita glasses. Colorful blobs encased in the clear material looked like confetti. They swirled and mixed in Devon's blurred vision. Last round for her. Being petite had been a curse she'd endured her entire life. Little to no tolerance for alcohol was a related inconvenience to suffer.

When Morgan finished serving them—all except Kate, who'd opted for fancy tea instead of booze—she plopped on the floor beside her best friend.

"So…" Kate leered at each of them in turn. "Truth or dare time."

"My favorite." Devon grinned.

"Good, then you first."

"Truth." She had no qualms about sharing herself with these women regardless of the silly game they played.

"Make it something juicy." Morgan poked Kate in the ribs. "You're evil at this. I should know. Remember when you forced me to admit my crush on your boyfriend in high school? Holy crap. I forgot his name. How can that be?"

"I think it was Tim. Or Ted maybe. Damn." Kate squinted. "It seemed like the end of the world at the time. Now that we have the crew, I can't help but think you saved me from potential disaster."

"Plus you got even in college with…" Morgan paused.

"Dan?"

"Uh, something like that. No, no, Doug. Definitely Doug." Morgan laughed. "I guess we've always had similar taste in guys."

"Great hormones think alike." Kate winked. "And now I *know* you've got it good with Joe."

"Lucky bitch." A slap on Kate's bared thigh accompanied the half-hearted curse.

"That's me. Anyhoo… It's been a while." Kate tapped her chin, then glanced at Kayla and Morgan. "I'm rusty. Help me. Both of you."

"Hell-oooo. You're the only sober one here." Kayla rolled her eyes. "You've got a pretty big advantage."

"Good point." Kate utilized their fit of giggles to consider. "Okay. But maybe we should change the rules. No singling anyone out. We'll all answer the question."

"Why the hell not?" Morgan shrugged. "We don't really believe in the whole solo thing around these parts. We're like the nine musketeers. Or is that three, three musketeers?"

"I can't do math after four margaritas!" Kayla rubbed her temples.

"You've had five," Kate corrected.

"You sort of proved her point." Devon nodded gingerly enough to avoid rattling her brains.

"Okay, okay." Kate held her hands up in surrender. "How about this? What's one thing you always hoped to try with our guys but haven't had the balls to go for yet?"

"Time to start planning our coup, huh?" Morgan *clinked* her glass against Kate's teacup.

"Yeah. I'll kick us off with some honesty of my own. Part of me is nervous. It's been a while now, coming up on two years, since I met the crew. I feel like we need to keep things fresh for Mike and the rest of them. They're used to adventure. I couldn't stand it if we didn't satisfy them as much as they've done for us." The rush with which the confession burst from Kate had them all sobering a tiny bit.

"You've thought about this a lot. Worried." Devon leaned forward to pat Kate's shoulder. "Mike adores you. You're all he really needs. You know that, right?"

"Yes." Kate swallowed hard enough for Devon to spot her throat flex. "I do. Deep down. That doesn't mean I don't want to give him the world. Better than only what he requires. Bare minimum isn't enough for the man of my dreams. We've also…"

"What, Katiebug?" Kayla defaulted to the nickname the guys had given their friend.

She released a dreamy sigh, then confessed, "Mike and I have toyed with starting a family."

"No wonder you're not drinking tonight." Kayla stared at the cup of tea clutched in Kate's white-knuckled grip.

"I've been dying to tell you all. I just..." She shook her head.

"You've been keeping too much inside." Morgan glared at Kate. "Don't you know we're here for you when you need us?"

"If we'd hidden something like this, you would have kicked our asses." Kayla leaned in closer. Morgan didn't harp, though. She glanced away, and her cheeks seemed to blush. Before Devon could dig deeper, Kate sighed.

"I know." At least she didn't attempt to deny it. "I'm sorry."

"So what's your main concern?" Devon tilted her head as she tried to decipher the issue.

"Once we have more responsibility, what if Mike is restless? As much as I can already feel a burning love for the baby we're praying for, I also know things will get harder. More stress. More obligation. More work. Our relationship could suffer. I'm terrified this brilliant magic we've created could fade into a perfectly comfortable, ordinary life. While he might be content, I can't imagine him happiest like that."

"Never forget we're a team." Morgan smirked. "With this many aunts and uncles to love a child, he or she won't be hard up for attention. And you'll never have to worry about a babysitter if you two need some time alone. Then, maybe someday, you could return the favor for Joe and me. Just think, our kids will grow up like brothers and sisters."

"That *is* nice to dream about." Kate brushed discreetly at the corner of her eye with a knuckle. "So I guess I'm going to answer my own stupid question. Tell me if I'm crazy."

"You are," Devon answered immediately.

"Brat." Kate's insult held no heat. Some of her seriousness dissolved. She took a deep breath, then admitted in a rush, "I'd like to watch one of you with Mike. I can't promise I won't get psycho jealous and try to rip you apart—gouge out your eyes or pull your hair or scratch you to shreds—but I'll do my best. I think he should have the option. And secretly, though he's never said anything, I think he's a touch jealous of the other guys. They got to be with some of you and he never did. Not that he wants to screw around or anything. But he's possessive. He considers all eight of us his in some way, you know?"

"You're both similar in that regard. Always taking care of the gang." Kayla grinned. "So how about a trade? Dave told me you were pretty damn hot that first time they shared you in the pool. I'm sure he'd be up for another taste. And he's plenty strong enough to keep your cat-fighting ninja moves in check should you make a break for me."

Devon noticed Morgan nodding in agreement. She thought about her relationship with the rest of the crew and how easy it would be to take the last step toward full-on intimacy. She loved each of the men for things they had in common as well as their individual strengths and quirks.

Morgan added softly, "I've grown so close to you all, and our guys. Most of us have been with some combination of them already...when we were first finding each other. One thing I've wondered about is making our sessions a free-for-all. The guys share each other. So why not us too? There are times, when we're all together, it would be so easy to reach out and touch Mike, Dave, Neil or James. They're gorgeous, and I love each of them. I'm sure I could improve their experience, same for them with me, but I'm afraid they're off limits. Why do we do that?"

Devon gnawed her lip. It was no secret Neil and James had played around with every one of her friends before she entered the picture. Truth be told, she imagined sometimes what it would have been like to be Kate. To have had all five men focused on her pleasure.

Greedy much? Hell, yeah.

She cleared the lump from her throat when no one spoke immediately. "Okay. I see your point. And I agree. None of us should be restricted. I trust you. You should do what comes naturally. If I'm being really honest, I'm envious of the time you had alone with the guys before I met you. Being the center of their attention had to rock. Sort of like Mike with you ladies, I've done the least playing with the crew."

"Holy shit." Kayla put her hand on Devon's knee and squeezed. "I never even considered you might feel like you missed out. Then again, you have two guys in your bed every night, so I don't have *too* much sympathy for you."

Another round of laughter broke out. Morgan nodded so vigorously she tipped off balance. Kate launched a potato chip in Devon's direction. Dev impressed herself by catching it in her mouth despite the alcohol dulling her reflexes. Useless skill #2184 learned in her years of working job sites filled with dudes, most of them a hell of a lot less evolved than the crew.

When they calmed down a little, Kayla continued, "Seriously, though, being with Dave, Neil and James is an experience I'll never forget. If you want that too, Dev, I'm fine with it. I think it would be hot to watch."

Devon's eyes grew wide when her friend—her worldly, open-minded, naturist friend—blushed bright red. "Um...and as for me, and the thing I'd like to try..."

Breath locked in Devon's lungs. She should have said something, done something, to encourage Kayla to continue. Instead, she froze.

"Uh oh. I think Morgan might be done." Kate poked their friend with her toe. She only mumbled and curled into a tighter ball on the floor. "Let's settle her on the couch before she's out cold. Otherwise, she'll regret it in the morning."

Together, the three of them managed to half-lift, half-coax Morgan onto the comfy, makeshift bed. Kate tucked a blanket around their sloshed friend, then fluffed a pillow to mitigate the awkward angle of her neck. Passing out like that all night would have guaranteed a strained muscle the next morning. Only once Morgan was set did Kate accept the quilt Kay furnished.

"I'll stay down here with her." She claimed her spot, reclining on the loveseat.

Disappointment rushed through Devon. Were they just going to abandon their discussion? Had things gone too far for her friends? They'd made some serious progress she would hate to erase. Maybe the other women had developed cold feet?

"It's okay, Dev." Kate reached out to pat her hip. "No one's going to change their mind between now and tomorrow. We'll finish our chat when everyone has a clear mind. Sleep well, girls."

"Thanks." Kayla smiled.

"Okay. You too, Kate." Devon wiggled her eyebrows. "Dirty dreams."

Morgan roused a bit when the lamp flicked off, leaving the glow from the dying fire as a soft nightlight. "Where they going? We're plog-ging."

"Plotting?"

"'S what I said. Blotting."

"Right. Well, we agree on the important stuff. Our plan of attack can wait until tomorrow," Kate reassured their friend. "Go to sleep."

As Devon followed Kayla toward the loft, she wondered if Kate realized what a great mom she'd make. She took a mental note to share her opinion when Kate couldn't blow off the compliment as an alcohol-induced warm fuzzy.

Not surprising, Morgan seemed to be on the same page. Devon caught a snippet of the best friends' whispered conversation while she and Kayla trekked up the steep, narrow loft stairs.

Morgan murmured to Kate, "Wow, a baby."

"I know. I'm freaked out and excited. Nervous to get my hopes up. We just started trying." She didn't pause to catch her breath as she rambled. "Maybe it won't happen for a while. Or ever. You know how much trouble my sister had..."

"Gonna be fine. Cutest kids ever, I bet." Their soft exchange drifted away as Devon entered Kayla's loft room. "Can't wait. Spoil 'em rotten..."

Kayla folded her thick down comforter to the foot of the bed and started to climb into the fluffy nest. Devon hopped onto the mattress and snuggled into the pile of pillows on Dave's side. When the other half didn't dip, she opened one eye and caught a shadow marking the spot where Kayla had paused.

"Kay?"

"Should I put pajamas on?" She sounded uncertain for the first time, maybe ever. "I can dig up one of Dave's T-shirts."

"If I can handle sitting in the stands while your husband fucks you—or my guys— senseless, I'm not about to turn squeamish about sleeping next to your bare tatas." She grunted. "Get your ass in here. These sheets are chilly."

Kayla didn't need to be asked twice. She slid beneath the covers but stayed so far away, Devon thought she'd tumble out the other side if she so much as sneezed. Stiff, awkward silence ballooned inside the loft, making it hard to catch her breath.

"What the hell is this crap?" Devon slapped a hand on Kayla's shoulder and tugged until her friend faced her.

"What?"

If Kayla intended to play dumb, Devon could do the same. Time to force them both to acknowledge the elephant in the room. Anything less would drive her batty before sunrise.

"You never did say what *you'd* like to try but haven't." Devon couldn't remember the last time she'd been coy in her life. Still, some tiny insecurity kept her from whispering her own desire into the night. The admission would have been so much easier if Neil and

James were there to coach her and hold her hand.

"Okay, fine. I think you know what I'm after," Kayla murmured. "When you're ready. *If* you ever are. All you have to do is say so. No pressure."

Devon grew warmer the instant she laid her hand on top of Kay's in the space between them. The other woman's pulse tripped against her own wrist before tapering to a more regular rhythm. Kayla sighed, and entwined their fingers. The bond they created transferred heat and reassurance that lulled them both to sleep in no time at all.

CHAPTER THREE

"**R**ise and shine, sleepyheads."

Devon groaned and burrowed closer to the warm body beside her without poking her head from beneath the jumble of covers. It wasn't until the racket caused by two people climbing the hardwood stairs roused her a little more that she realized the person snuggled up to her was soft in all the places her guys were hard. *Mmm, nice.*

"Kayla."

"Yeah, I'm awake." Her clear voice didn't seem to indicate she'd been jerked out of a wonderful dream about sexy, naked construction workers mere seconds earlier either. How long had she been lying there, thinking?

"Damn. What time is it?" Devon blinked in rapid succession. She squinted into the unusually refulgent morning sunlight as she attempted to shove onto a straight-locked arm while clutching the sheets to her bare chest. She blew rogue strands of hair from her face.

"Almost noon," Kate informed them. She set a tall glass of orange juice on the nightstand, then towered over Devon and Kayla. "I couldn't let you miss out on the chance for one of Morgan's amazing breakfasts. She made waffles from scratch, the kind with fruit and her secret spices in them."

Devon sniffed the air. "Oh my God. Do I smell bacon too?"

"Could be." Morgan grinned. She set a tray of food carefully on the nightstand.

"Hold that thought. If I don't pee right now, I'm going to drown." Devon scampered from the bed. Less than a minute later she bounded to the loft once more.

Kayla, Morgan and Kate held congress in low tones from their perches on the rumpled duvet.

"No, nothing happened..." Kay bit her lip and hesitated when she caught sight of Devon returning.

"What's going on?" Dev asked.

"We're waiting for you to get your act together so we can savor our feast." Kate deflected genuine concern with sarcasm. "So hurry it up, punk."

"Oh yeah? I'll give you *punk*." Devon sprinted the last few feet. She leaped and tucked her knees to her chest, cannonballing into the pile of plush covers between her friends. The mattress bounced, jostling them all.

"Very funny." Kayla laughed as she whipped a pillow from the head of the bed. "But you left yourself unprotected."

Whap.

Something puffy smashed into her face. "You did not just hit me with…"

Whap. Whap.

Kate and Morgan joined in the battle. They took turns pummeling her with the light bundles. Devon's fit of giggles didn't do much for her coordination. She lunged for the fourth pillow while unsuccessfully attempting to evade the incoming barrage.

Battling to her knees on the mattress allowed her to launch a counterstrike. Her one-against-three odds improved when her friends' coalition deteriorated. They whacked each other as often as they did her. Every woman for herself.

They shrieked, chased, ducked, whooped, dove, tackled and smacked each other. Feathers flew through the air. They fell as thick as the flakes that had blanketed the mountain during the legendary blizzard that fused Dave and Kayla in an inseparable pair the previous winter. Busy daydreaming about what it would have been like to watch Dave, James and Neil ravaging Kay in front of the fireplace downstairs, Devon got caught off guard.

Whap.

She leaned into the force of the blow, but it was no use. Her arms windmilled. Gravity pitched her inevitably toward the floor. She braced herself for impact, heart racing as she completed a split-second assessment of the minimalist railing that kept the space open to the cabin below. It would probably hold.

Instead of a slat of wood to the ribs, strong arms—too thick to belong to one of her female friends—banded around her.

Neil. She would recognize his hold anywhere. A perfect blend of tender yet unbreakable.

"It's all fun and games until someone cracks their skull open." He rocked Devon against his chest. "Careful, baby. I have plans for today that don't involve a trip to the emergency room."

"Unless it's because you've fucked yourself into complete exhaustion and dehydration, right?" Joe smacked Neil's back, rattling both him and Devon.

She hated that she nearly cried. Clawing at Neil's shoulders, she encouraged him to squeeze her tighter. "You're home early! Damn, I missed you."

"Same goes. Couldn't stay away any longer." He buried his nose in her hair and breathed deep.

"What the hell is going on in here?" Mike asked as the rest of the crew piled in close on Neil's heels.

The loft had never seemed cramped before. Hard bodies and testosterone overwhelmed Devon's senses. She couldn't speak so she indulged in the luxury of having them surround her.

"A pillow fight?" Dave groaned when he took in the four women, naked except for the feathers tangled in their hair and stuck to the light sheen of perspiration coating their flushed skin. They breathed hard where they'd collapsed onto the bed. "And here I thought you couldn't get any sexier."

"Why the hell did we need a vacation again? We're living the dream." Joe stared, licking his lips, while James sidled up beside Neil. He sandwiched Devon between their chests. Neil angled her so she faced their partner. Several inches shorter than Neil, he easily claimed her mouth in a scorching yet infinitely tender kiss. His fingertip traced the tattoo—similar to the one both he and Neil sported—on her ring finger.

"I missed you too," Devon whispered when they finally broke apart.

"But not as much as Kay missed me. Right, babe?" Dave strutted to the side of the bed near his wife.

Morgan surprised them all when she whacked him hard in the gut with her pillow. "Ha! She's got nothing on me. Without Joe, I almost died of loneliness. And horniness."

The women's ceasefire erupted into a second round of good-natured exchanges. Devon squirmed from Neil's arms to join the fray. The crew cheered on their girls, calling out helpful tips. When Kate swung wide, her pillow caught the edge of the tray on the nightstand.

Mike dove for the tipping platter. The guys roared when he rescued it. Sort of like he'd done for Kate that fateful afternoon two summers ago.

"Hey, now. Truce. That's not funny. Bacon almost became an innocent casualty. Wasting it would be a cardinal sin. Straight to hell, do not pass go." Joe snapped up a slice and devoured it in one bite. If he were a cartoon, they would have heard the *galoomp* of him swallowing it whole.

"Did you even chew that?" James shook his head, whether in awe or disgust it was hard to tell.

"There's nothing better than salty breakfast meat."

"That's what *he* said." Kayla had her friends rolling with her snide interjection.

As if they were universally wired, the guys scanned first the pile of steaming waffles, then the assortment of women. They made the circuit several times. Dave practically gave himself whiplash before growling, "We can reheat the food when we're finished working up our appetites."

"No bacon left behind," Mike agreed.

"I'm dying for a taste of you." Joe rushed Morgan. He triggered a stampede.

The crew invaded the girls' sanctuary, pairing—or trebling—up with their mates. Moans and sighs replaced battle cries as they held sensual reunions.

Devon gasped when Neil pressed her to the bed. A welter of limbs cascaded over her as nine people found a way to share the king-sized bed in some fashion or another. They writhed in the wake of equal pleasure.

"I have a better idea." James lifted his head from where he'd suckled Devon's nipple into a taut peak. "No reason we can't have our women and eat them too."

"I like the way you think." Dave groaned. "Hand me some of that whipped cream."

Neil's hand shook as he passed the gravy boat heaped with fresh-made topping. The cobalt glass slipped from his grip. Joe snagged the handle, keeping the vessel from bonking Kayla. The rapid deceleration launched the contents all over. Splatter dispersed across Kate, Mike, Kayla, Devon and anyone else in the path of the sweet cream.

"Shit." Neil's pupils dilated when a glob dripped off James's pec onto Devon's tummy.

Before she could register the chill accompanying the splash above her mound, the moist heat of Neil's tongue swiped across the same spot. All too soon, he'd licked her clean.

"Excuse me." James grinned as he slipped his hand past Dave, who'd crawled between his wife's legs for the best seat in the house at the unusual buffet.

Kayla arched. Each of the men scooped a portion of the treat from her skin.

"You like them petting you?" Dave murmured against the succulent flesh of her pussy.

"Yes. God, yes." She spread her legs wider, rocking her hips toward her husband's parted lips. "Eat me."

He did.

Devon observed the industrious man devouring her friend. He made up in gusto anything he might have lacked in finesse. Long laps of his tongue gathered whipped cream mixed with the glistening arousal spreading across Kayla's inner thigh.

Neil groaned. Devon's fingers clenched on his shoulders, urging him closer. He obliged her unspoken command by lavishing similar attention on her.

James wormed into an available space between Devon and Morgan. The entire loft overflowed with passionate cries and hard-bodied males worshipping their women. He rolled onto his side, his cock prodding the curve of her hip as he settled his lips over hers for a series of sinful kisses. His mouth tasted faintly of vanilla.

He burrowed one arm beneath her neck, supporting her head. He held her at the angle he preferred for feasting on her lips. Their tongues flicked over one another. His detoured to trace the corners of her smile and tickle the roof of her mouth. They alternated ravenous sucks with dainty sips.

She shivered when Neil thrust his firm tongue into the opening of her pussy. Her hands glided upward, burying in the almost-too-long strands of Neil's thick hair.

"Dev, if *you're* touching him..." James angled his head to verify she hadn't shifted as he murmured to her. Before he could sort out the puzzle, his brains understandably addled by the outrageous level of pheromones battering their systems, Morgan came to his rescue.

"Hey there, cutie." Morgan winked before tugging on James's erection.

"Um." His stare flew between Devon, Neil, Joe and Mike to gauge their reactions. "Am I allowed to enjoy this?"

Mike shrugged. "Why do I get the feeling we should have known better than to leave these vixens to find trouble without us?"

"It's okay with me." Devon grinned.

"Joe?" James stayed stock still.

"Shit, it's hot. If my wife wants to jerk you off, I vote for letting her. She passes inspection in my book when it comes to hand jobs."

The other crew members groaned.

"Alrighty then." James clamped his fingers around Morgan's, which were slick with whipped cream, encouraging her to stroke faster.

"Well, since we're playing like that..." Mike swiped a dollop of fluff from Kayla's chest, lingering longer than necessary to massage some of it into the swell of her breast. He walked his fingers up her neck and allowed her to suck his index finger clean.

"Yeah, that's right, sweetheart." His hand shook as Kate straddled him, grinding on his obvious hard-on. Only then did Devon realize the guys were naked. They must have shed their standard jeans and T-shirt uniforms on arrival at Kay's naturist retreat. She certainly didn't intend to complain about the display of cut muscles and sleek bodies.

"Neil." She whimpered his name several times before her plea registered.

"Dev?" He glanced up though he didn't stop teasing her for longer than it took to whisper her name.

"Will you fuck me? Please. Need you inside me."

"No." He shook his head, causing the nerves in her swollen folds to riot. "But I will make love to you. Here. With our friends surrounding us. Joining in."

Devon smiled when she thought about sharing the positive energy they generated. She'd been hanging around Kayla and her New Age junk too much lately.

James reached for Neil's cock when their lover rose over her. The smaller man guided their mate's long erection to her opening. The slickness the men inspired ensured Neil glided through her rings of muscle despite the tight fit he still made with her body.

"You love watching them together." Morgan didn't ask James. She didn't have to with her fingers wrapped around his steely shaft. "I swear you just got twice as hard, and that's saying something."

"Yeah." He groaned.

"And you. You're soaked." Joe snuggled tight to Morgan's back. With her front pressed to James, she could have felt claustrophobic. Her guttural moan proved that wasn't the case. "You like being a dirty girl, don't you? What does it feel like to grope my friend while I'm fucking you?"

"Gah!"

Kate chuckled at Morgan's helplessness. Grunts and sighs fell from the couple. Joe draped Morgan's knee over James's hip to guarantee he'd penetrated her completely.

Devon tried to watch. Flat on her back, she missed some of the action.

"Here, shorty." Neil scooped one arm beneath her shoulders without a hitch in his stride. He rocked into her as he rearranged some of the pillows, inclining her shoulders until she could survey the entire lascivious landscape.

Despite only sixty-seven and a half hours apart, she could tell he worked harder to penetrate her than he had when he'd said goodbye. Luckily, the visuals turned her on even more. She appreciated the distraction from slight discomfort that quickly became something entirely pleasurable.

"We can't all be giants like you." She nipped Neil's bottom lip before he rose to optimize the angle of his stokes. With the view clear, she allowed her gaze to wander.

She lay on her back with Neil pumping into her, making her see more stars than the night sky held far out here on the top of the mountain. James lounged on his side facing her. Morgan's hand brushed the dip of her waist and the side of her ribs as she worked the gentle man who'd captured Devon's heart from her very first day as the crew's intern.

She paused to stare into his eyes, which looked so much like her own it startled her on occasion.

"I love you," he moaned before stretching his neck toward her for another taste. Neil swooped in to lick the seam of their mouths. Soon the three of them traded open-mouthed kisses.

When they came up for air, Devon continued to feed off the scene before her. Beyond James, Morgan took Joe's increasing strokes, writhing between the men bracketing her. The roving action of her hand on James's cock grew less regular. James facilitated the exchange by fucking into her hold. The ruddy tip of his hard-on poked Devon in the side at the apex of each thrust.

Beyond the three lovers on their sides, Mike reclined, stretched out like a sultan enjoying his harem. With his arms crossed behind his head, he held himself in a suspended crunch as though it were no effort at all. With ripped abs like his, maybe it wasn't.

"Like what you see?" He smirked when he caught her staring.

Kate must have read Devon's mind. She tweaked her husband's nipple. The cocky foreman jerked, rubbing the sting from his chest even as he laughed. Still, his raging erection never wilted.

"Behave yourself." Kate wagged her index finger at him. He rocked upward to catch it in his mouth, sucking until his wife melted a tiny bit.

"I could say the same for you." He dusted light kisses over her knuckles between every couple words. "But I'd much rather you be naughty. Quit teasing me. Three days is too long to be without you. Put my cock inside you. Now."

Devon shivered at the command inherent in his tone. Mike was impossible to resist when he got bossy.

Kate lifted up to make room for his shaft. She braced herself on his chest with one hand, the other reaching behind her blindly. Devon couldn't fault her for the lack of coordination that had her fishing for Mike's cock. The surfeit of sexy men would make anyone's system go haywire.

Kayla noticed Kate's dilemma and lent a helping hand. Cleaned of the cream, she rolled from her back and swiped at the last blob, which decorated the corner of Dave's mouth, with one finger. From where she perched on her hands and knees at the foot of the bed, she extended her left hand. Perpendicular to the three other couples, she easily encircled the base of Mike's shaft with her long fingers.

"I've got this, Kate." Kayla moaned when Dave couldn't resist the temptation of her ass on display before him. The broadest and most powerful of them all, he made sure not to crush anyone's legs when he scrambled to kneel behind his wife. The colorful design of her alluring tattoos flexed as she settled herself. They provided the perfect lines for Dave to trace with his tongue.

James, Morgan and Joe shuffled their feet and legs so they rested on top of Dave's calves, ankles and soles. They anchored him to the bed.

Each of them was connected in some way to the rest of the crew.

Kay still rode the same mental wavelength as Devon. She glanced up from her task, meeting Dev's stare.

How had they ended up as far away as possible from each other in the intertwined knot of lovers? Despite Kayla's lissome frame, enhanced by attending the early morning yoga sessions her resort offered, there was no way she and Devon could touch from opposite corners of the enormous bed.

Devon couldn't justify the sliver of disappointment prickling her heart.

James murmured, "What's wrong?"

"Nothing, really."

"You'll tell me later, right?" He whispered in her ear, so no one else heard.

She nodded.

He issued comfort in the form of a soft sweep of his lips down her cheek, along her jaw, then over her mouth. She reveled in the lingering taste of the whipped cream before shifting her attention to her friends once more.

Kayla had resumed her post, aligning the fat head of Mike's cock. Her hand slipped between Kate's thighs, ensuring she'd estimated the angle correctly. Kate and Mike both groaned at the flutter of skilled fingers over their aching genitals.

The constant pressure Neil imparted to Devon's channel as he filled her nudged her close to the edge of ecstasy. Devon could relate to the wild cries Kate unleashed when she slid down Mike's shaft, impaling herself on his full length. Kayla lowered her hand, fondling Mike's tight sac with a gentle caress that made Devon pretty damn sure her friend also remembered their conversation from the night before.

What if they all were together when Kate and Mike started their family?

"Shit, yes," the foreman hissed at the dual sensation of his wife sheathing him and their friend cupping his balls. He collapsed onto the mattress, his shoulders and head bouncing a little following the thud. His hands surrounded Kate's hips. Dinged, calloused fingers splayed across her ass.

He encouraged her to ride him, setting a demanding pace she eagerly complied with.

Kayla shouted when Dave distracted her from her ministrations by plunging his cock to the hilt in her welcoming body with one complete stroke. He covered her back, biting her shoulder as he fondled her breasts with his large hands. The graceful ripple of his body as he fucked Kay mesmerized Devon.

Did Neil look like that as he took her?

She looked into his wide eyes and flushed face. He must have read the desire there.

"That hot, huh?"

"Yeah," was all she could manage.

"Good thing I can't see them. I wouldn't last thirty seconds. It's hard enough listening to them. Sinking inside you. Christ. You feel so good."

Devon's legs spread as wide as they could, inviting him deeper, given her precarious spot on the edge of the bed and the pile of bodies to her left. James ducked his head to torture her breast. He sucked on her, bit her gently and plumped the modest mound with one hand while the other snaked lower to her pussy.

The industrious glide of Morgan's fingers over his cock freed him to pay the pleasure forward to Devon. His hand danced over her mound, glancing across her clit before measuring Neil's girth where he spread her pussy wide open.

James gathered moisture from the intersection of Devon and Neil's bodies. He used the slickness to draw frictionless circles around the hooded knot of her clit. Neil echoed her shudder when her pussy clamped tighter on his hard-on.

"You're strangling me," he rasped. "Come when you can, Dev."

"No." She thrashed her head on the pillow. "Not without the rest of you."

"You're so sweet." Joe reached past Morgan to pat Devon's tummy. "No one minds, munchkin. Hell. Likely to set us all off."

Devon scrunched her eyes closed, trying to regain a measure of control. It was no use. Neil descended. He trapped James's palm over her mound. The suction of Neil's mouth on the far side of her chest mimicked James's attention on her right breast, stealing the last of her reason.

She surrendered to pure sensation.

Devon relaxed, absorbing the pummeling of Neil's hips. The steady tap pressed James's wiggling fingers right where she needed the contact most. She resisted the initial wave of pleasure battering her senses. But when she made the mistake of opening her eyes, she caught sight of the admiration and lust in Kayla's.

The link was too much on top of all the other stimulation.

Devon's gaze winged frantically from person to person, trying to include them all in the moment. Each crew member focused on her as if they sensed her impending capitulation.

"Let go, Dev," Mike ordered. "We're with you."

An orgasm the likes of which she'd never experienced before wrung her dry from the inside out. It started as a buzz deep in her core and expanded until even her fingertips sang with ultimate pleasure. She'd swear her hair stood on end as electricity raced through her veins.

"Yes. Fuck." Neil threw his head back and roared. The tendons in his neck stood out in relief on the powerful column. They looked like the veins and ridges of his cock felt caressing her spasming tissue. "Me too."

"Fill her," James encouraged their lover. "Show her how you wouldn't let me take care of you while we were away. You tried to tease me. Backfired, didn't it? Give her everything you saved up."

If Neil wasn't the absolute picture of health, Devon might have worried about him keeling over. His heart hammered against her palm when she lifted it to his chest. Still she unraveled, and he rode her through the never-ending pulses of her climax.

"Yes. Yes. Yes," Neil chanted.

The first jet of his semen shot within her, splattering on the swollen walls of her pussy. He grunted and jerked between her thighs over and over, emptying himself with a ferocity she didn't often witness from her playful lover. The stakes had been raised again. Each person's rapture amplified as it fed off that of their neighbor, friend, paramour and confidant too.

"That's it." James cheered them both on. He tapped a secret code on her clit that never failed to set her ablaze. "Wring him dry."

Neil huffed as though he'd run an entire marathon in those sixty seconds. He rocked onto his haunches, looking unsteady and utterly wrecked. Dave put out a hand to steady his partner without pausing his beat as he fucked his wife. In fact, the contact might have been responsible for him speeding up his pace a tad.

Kayla moaned and lowered her cheek to Mike's shin. She gripped his ankle with her right hand. Head down, ass up, she accepted everything Dave had to give her. Still, the fingers of her left hand drew swirling patterns over Mike's balls, massaging them.

Kate bounced on her husband's shaft, somehow managing to look graceful as always despite the primal forces possessing her and obliterating all traces of the proper lady she pretended to be at times.

Aftershocks zinged through Devon, enhanced by the saturnalia around her and the calming strokes of Neil's palm over her arms, chest and belly. When she emerged from the daze of the most powerful climax of her life, she didn't waste any time. She yanked Neil toward her for a sloppy kiss before zeroing her focus on James.

"I like the way you think, Dev." Neil added his caresses to the exposed form of their lover.

Now petted by six hands, maybe more if she counted the occasional touches from Joe, James had no chance at resistance. He made a final stand, locking his jaw so tight she worried he'd crack a molar.

She grinned into his gorgeous eyes.

"Oh shit." He gasped at the dirty intentions in her gaze.

Devon reached over and rubbed his nipples with the sharp flicks destined to set him off. Sure enough, the scrape of her nails over the pebbled discs had him seizing in Morgan's embrace.

Come blasted from his cock, catching Devon and Neil with the spray. More fluid dripped from the head to coat Morgan's fingers as she stroked him slow and sweet after the initial rush had burst free. She massaged his softening flesh, bringing him down gently.

James sighed, welcoming first Neil's, then Devon's mouth on his. When they'd had their fill of his lips, he tipped his head, letting Morgan decide if she'd like to accept his invitation.

She did.

Devon smiled as the other woman moaned into James's mouth.

"Oh shit, yeah," Joe shouted as he fucked his wife harder. He examined her kissing James up close and personal. "You're going to make her come, James. She likes it when you suck on her tongue."

James must have obliged. His throat flexed, and a keening wail escaped from Morgan's chest. Devon stroked her hair while Mike crooned to her from behind the couple. Devon couldn't understand the individual words, but the tone conveyed all she needed to know.

Morgan bucked between James and Joe, surrendering to their spell. Joe stiffened and cursed a blue streak. He often did when he lost total control. Mike and Kate joined their friends, all four of them filling the loft with clear signs of their pleasure.

"That's so hot," Kayla panted from her front row seat. "I can see. Mike. Overflowing."

Devon couldn't quite tell what Kay did then. Both Mike and Kate yelled, their orgasms extending at the contact. She figured it out soon enough when Dave groaned. He captured his wife's wrist, then tugged it behind her back. He lunged forward, enveloping her fingers in his mouth, sucking the combined flavor of Mike and Kate from them.

The restraint of her arm and the knowledge of how much Dave had shared seemed to push Kayla off the precipice. She clutched Mike's leg with her free hand and might have toppled beneath the force of Dave's enthusiastic fucking if it hadn't been for Joe, who sat up and braced her.

Dave tightened his grip on her ass, slamming home as Kayla shook and moaned. The periodic clenching of his glutes as he released inside his wife fascinated Devon. She wished she could pet his flank as he spilled his seed deep in Kayla's pussy. Neil reached out and did it for her.

For long minutes they all lay silent except for the rasp of their breathing and an occasional moan that refused to be muted. Content, Devon could have stayed floating in that cloud of mutual admiration and bliss for the rest of her life.

"Welcome home." Kayla nuzzled Dave, who'd sank on top of her, trapping her to their bed where she seemed perfectly happy remaining for the foreseeable future.

Devon adjusted to make room for Neil. She sat with her shoulders propped against the headboard, cradling Neil's and James's cheeks in her palms. They rested their heads on her thighs. Someone's stomach growled so loud she might have thought it was a truck in the driveway if she didn't know better.

She leaned to the side and plucked a slice of bacon from the tray. She held the strip between her guys, grinning when they ate it *Lady and the Tramp* style. Their lips locked when they reached the center, thrillingly close to her pussy.

"I could go for some of that too."

Devon passed the plate to Kate, who selected a waffle quarter. She ripped off a piece for herself, then another to pop into Mike's open mouth. He licked melted butter from her fingers before chewing his treat.

Soon, they all were indulging in a decadent breakfast in bed. Sporadic yawns ensured naptime was next on the agenda. Curled together, no one would be left in the cold as they dreamed of new ways to play with each other that would be hard pressed to surpass reality.

When they'd all settled in, satisfied, Joe announced to the room in general, "I take it back. We should definitely go away more often."

All four women bashed him with their pillows.

CHAPTER FOUR

Morgan fiddled with the whisk attachment on the stand mixer she'd bought for Kayla's kitchen. She baked here often enough to justify the gadget. Meanwhile, Mike finished the last bite of his third helping of the passion-fruit crepes she'd whipped up in the aftermath of their sharing to help refuel the crew.

The extravagant breakfast for four she'd started out with seemed paltry when faced with the five bottomless pits the guys called stomachs. They could easily plow through enough food to keep her in business for eternity. They also loved helping her refine her experiments for Sweet Treats.

"What's the verdict?" She crossed her fingers.

"Fucking great." Mike thought for a minute, attempting to flesh out his description, as if knowing it'd help her understand the dish's potential. "Love how it's crunchy on the outside and squishy in the center. The plainer part helps temper the goo on top. It's crazy sweet. Love it."

Okay, so they had a little way to go yet before she'd claim to have trained them as panel tasters. She laughed. "Thanks."

He leaned against the cabinets, shooting the shit with her between delighting his tastebuds and complimenting the chef. Joe and Kate weren't quite ready to head back into town. Steam billowed from the bathroom where Kate showered, and Joe hadn't roused from his mandatory post-orgy nap. He loved the deep slumber following great sex so much, Morgan didn't have the heart to wake him just yet. Even if their pillow fight had aggravated the paring knife stabbing through her eye socket courtesy of her indulgence the night before. She smiled as she peeked at her husband, crashed on the couch in the adjoining room. When he was near, all her aches evaporated.

A hiss drew her attention back to Mike. He cleared his throat and attempted to disguise his wince as he swallowed the final morsel, complete with extra syrup from the edges of the plate.

Morgan crossed to him, relieving him of the dirty dish. "You know, that's only going to keep getting worse if you don't go to the dentist. Better have it taken care of before it turns into a fiasco."

"Shit." He massaged his jaw, as if that would help. "Don't mention it to Kate, okay? How could you tell?"

"When you drank the cold OJ with your first pass at breakfast, you flinched." She rubbed his shoulder, hoping to grant him some comfort. It seemed so natural to touch him, although the gesture had nothing sexual about it.

"Damn Joe's cousins." He scowled. "They're wild bastards, I swear. We need to find them some fine women to settle them down a bit."

She cocked her head, wondering what the Carter clan had to do with this.

"They were giving us shit about getting domesticated." He at least had the sense to look ashamed. "We'd had a *few* too many beers while waiting for nonexistent fish to bite."

"You got in a fist fight?" Morgan's eyes grew wide.

"It wasn't as barbaric as you make it sound." He shrugged. "Just a little roughhousing among friends. Except my boot slipped on the ice and I smacked my jaw pretty hard on Logan Carter's tackle box. I think I might have cracked one of my molars.

Son of a bitch. I hate the dentist. *Really* hate it."

Morgan had never seen Mike like this before. His foot wiggled non-stop while his fingers beat an erratic tattoo on the counter.

Every superman had his kryptonite.

"Hey." She put her arms around his waist and hugged him. "I completely understand. I'm really afraid of the dentist too."

He shot her a look just short of rolling his eyes. "A lot of people dislike it. I get that, but I can't explain how it makes me feel. Something along the lines of a chick screaming on top of a table when a mouse invades her kitchen. It's irrational and stupid. I still can't help it."

"You mean how your heart seizes up like you're going to die, or how your vision narrows into tiny pinpricks of light, or how you can't draw a full breath into your lungs?" She shivered.

"Yeah. Like that." He frowned. "Didn't you get crowns on your front teeth last year? How the hell did you manage that if you're as scared as I am?"

"I didn't the first three times. I pulled into the lot and drove right back home." She couldn't say which of them clutched the other tighter.

"Why the hell didn't you say something?" He hugged her to him and sighed.

"I was embarrassed." She grimaced.

"So how did you work up the guts to go through with it?" He paused. "Did it hurt this bad? And you suffered? Shit, better not tell Joe that. Soon I'm not going to be able to fall asleep. It throbs like a motherfucker."

"Yeah, there was that, although mine was more cosmetic at this stage. Plus, I went to school with a guy who's a dentist these days. Graduated at the top of his class, I swear. He has a fancy practice in the converted farmhouse on Werner Avenue. When I balked, he fetched me from the bakery."

"Nick Rocha?" Mike held her away a bit so he could meet her gaze.

"Yeah. You know him too?" She smiled.

"Sort of. We did the work on the building."

"I've always liked the way it turned out. The circular windows are my favorite."

"Blame your husband for that. He insisted they'd be perfect even though they were a pain in the ass to install and put us over budget." Mike smiled, some of his anxiety fading away.

"I wouldn't lie to you. He's good. Gentle. And he has lots of new-fangled gadgets to make procedures quicker and less painful than you're probably used to." She paused to consider. "He even offers oral sedation if you'd rather zone out while he's doing his thing. I don't mind driving you. Between both of us, I'm sure we could convince him to fit you in soon so you don't have to stress out."

Mike shuddered but nodded. "Fine. But I think I need you to make the call. Otherwise, I'll probably turn chickenshit again."

"No problem." She squeezed his hand, surprised by how sweaty yet icy it was. "Everyone's afraid of something, Mike."

"I guess." He wiped his palms on his jeans. "Thanks for noticing and for offering to hold my hand. Even though it'll be gross and slimy then too."

"What's the point of being a team if we don't each bring something to the game?" She smiled softly. "You're welcome."

***

"Joe?" Morgan sat up. She thought she'd heard a rattle from the general direction of the bathroom. Dusk permitted her a shadowy glimpse into the space adjoining their bedroom. "Everything okay?"

She didn't remember much of the ride home from Kayla and Dave's house this afternoon. She'd conked out before they'd emerged from the woods surrounding the resort's long, winding driveway. Head still pounding from the night before and their wild romp—though she wouldn't have missed out on that for the world—she'd surrendered to the utter relaxation suffusing her at having her man by her side again. Not to mention the boneless state their group session had put her in.

Grateful for the stress reduction, she'd embraced the floating sensation and let Joe's crooning duets with his favorite, Michael Bublé, via the streaming radio on his smartphone lull her into oblivion. A vague memory of him carrying her up the stairs to their apartment over the bakery, tucking her into their bed, inflated her heart to greater proportions.

The pressure had her chest aching when she remembered the bad news she had to tell him. No more excuses. It wasn't right to let him hang on to false hope.

Vile cursing followed a second, louder metallic clank.

She padded to the doorway, leaned on the jamb and admired the muscles in her husband's bare shoulders. They bunched and stretched from his place beside the toilet. He'd removed the lid of the tank to fiddle with something inside. He shook his hand, then mummified it in toilet paper. If she had to guess, she'd say he stanched blood welling from yet another gouge in his poor, battered fingers.

"What's up?"

"Damn. Tried not to wake you. Sorry." He swiped a bead of sweat from his brow with the side of his forearm. The motion left a grease streak that only enhanced his rugged charm. A spike of his golden hair stuck to the stain. "Thought I'd install the new valve and flange I picked up for this guy so it'll stop running in the middle of the night."

"Thanks, you know that drives me bonkers. Hate to waste water." Morgan frowned.

"Yeah, your Mother Earth act is cute even when it's a royal pain in the ass." Joe didn't flinch when she smacked his shoulder playfully.

"Hey, what's that?" She leaned in for a closer look, then clapped her hands. "You found a handle to match the sink hardware?"

"It was supposed to be a surprise." He grimaced. "I almost finished. But my hand slipped and I busted my knuckles on the nut. Hurt like a motherfucker."

"That's what *he* said," Morgan muttered under her breath.

"What?" Joe cocked his head.

"Nothing. Sorry. Kayla's a bad influence." She returned her attention to the vintage blue and white porcelain handle, admiring the intricate floral pattern all over again. Gorgeous. Classic. It matched the sink set she'd picked up at one of the antique malls she frequented with Kate. The embellishment couldn't have been easy to find. God only knew how many specialty websites he'd surfed or stores he'd called. What other man would pay attention to such a tiny detail?

"You like it?"

"It's perfect. Thank you." She looked up, admiring his bare chest and feet. She kissed his cheek, then daubed the perspiration trickling from his temple to his jaw with the tail of the long shirt he must have changed her into. "Your surprises will never get old."

"Even when they cut your nap short?" Joe finished tinkering with the guts of the tank, replaced the lid and waved to the handle. "Do the honors. Give it a test flush."

She did, raving over his upgrades.

"Thank you, thank you." He issued her a mock bow as he climbed to his feet. Suddenly the bathroom seemed to shrink. His heat and powerful build filled the space.

"And yes, being woken up is well worth it when it means a man as sexy as you is on his knees, servicing my appliances."

He leveled a searing stare in her direction.

Her legs went weak.

Joe scanned her from her tousled hair to the wrinkled flannel shirt she'd filched from his drawer and worn each night he was absent. He licked his lips.

"I don't think my wife would appreciate the way you're staring at me, ma'am." He returned her grin with interest.

Had any man ever been as fine as him? Playful yet smoking hot, he turned her insides as mushy as the fruit she'd macerated for the filling in tomorrow's daily special—a mixed berry pie.

"Give me ten minutes and I'll make you forget all about her." Morgan stalked the step or two to Joe, employing her best imitation of a sultry swagger. She ran the tip of one finger from the hollow of his neck through the smattering of his light chest hair, along the valley separating his rock-hard abs. When she landed on the waistband of his jeans, she skimmed his trim sides until she slipped her hands into his back pockets.

A double handful of his tight ass acted as a convenient grip to tug him closer. The ridge of his cock pressed into her belly. He stiffened a little, putting her at arm's length so he could stare point-blank into her eyes.

"You didn't answer my question, cupcake." He wiped his hands on his denim-clad thighs before he traced the dark circles beneath her eyes with his thumbs. "You were out like a light. Tired for a reason?"

She stared at the black and white tiled floor he'd installed last summer until he lifted her chin with one of his bandage-free knuckles.

"Morgan?"

"I got my period the morning you left. It was a false alarm." She bit the inside of her cheek. "I'm so sorry."

"Shush." He rubbed her lower back with his undamaged hand, which nearly spanned her waist, and kissed her nose. "Nothing to apologize for. I should have been here. I knew you were late… Hoping…"

"I'm sorry I didn't say so right away. I couldn't stand to disappoint you again." She rested her head on his shoulder. Maybe he'd think the moisture tracking down his chest was the result of a few more droplets of sweat instead of the tears she shed.

"Never." He hugged her tight.

"And then last night, I got drunk. Really hammered." She hiccupped. So much for stealth weeping. "I couldn't bring myself to say it out loud. You know, like then it would be real. I had to forget about it for a while and I knew it was safe. I passed out because I was hungover, not because I'm pregnant. So sorry."

"Ah, honey, you should have called me home." He rocked her against his chest.

"Why?" She sighed. "Nothing you could do."

"You never have to suffer alone." He finger-combed her hair. "Seriously, Morgan, that's a major benefit of our crew. I'm sure they'll look after you if I can't for some reason. It's one of the things that makes me comfortable leaving. Why didn't you confide in Dev, Kate and Kayla? They would have been there for you."

"I know. I almost did last night. Then Kate told us that her and Mike are trying too."

"He mentioned it to us on the trip." Joe nodded.

"Well, you know how much trouble Kate's sister had. Another rocky experience wasn't what she needed to hear about." Morgan clung to her husband, so glad to have him home, here, in her arms. "Psyching her out isn't going to help."

"Maybe you need to take your own advice, Mo." He made a circuit up her spine, then down her sides with his sure fingers. "Getting upset isn't going to help matters. A bunch of the books we read said it's normal for it to take up to a year of trying. Let's enjoy each other. The rest will take care of itself."

"You're right." She drew a deep breath, then blurted, "But I think we should make an appointment to have some tests done. Fertility and genetics stuff."

"Okay, sure." He rubbed their noses together. "Probably not a bad idea in any case."

"You *hate* the doctor. Sor—"

"Don't you dare apologize again. I'd do anything for you." He kissed her long and slow until her toes curled in the bathmat and ten tons lifted off her shoulders. "I'd hope you'd understand that by now. Fucking *anything* to make you smile."

"No one does that as well as you." She encircled his waist with her arms and nuzzled her cheek against the hard planes of his chest. "I love you, Joe."

"Same goes." He ruffled her hair.

"So, how about we take a shower together and practice, huh?" She nipped his pec. "Another week or so and we'll be in primetime again."

"I'm not sure that's a good idea." He stared into her eyes with more seriousness than she could ever remember.

"You want to give up already? I can handle this. I thought—"

"I meant the wasted water." He covered her mouth with a searing kiss. After nibbling on her bottom lip, he retreated with a smirk. "This could be an awfully long shower if we do it right."

"Some things are worth the sacrifice." Morgan reached in to flip on the spray. "Oh my God. You found matching shower fixtures, too?"

"Nah." He shook his head. "They never produced them compatible with this type of plumbing."

"Then how?" She stared at him like he was her hero, because he was.

"My cousin Eli has some fabrication connections for the parts they use in fixing up classic cars." He grinned. "Probably the first time he's asked them to make shower handles and toilet hardware instead. Those bastards had a field day ripping on me."

"You really are full of surprises." She knelt before him to tear open his button fly.

His jeans pooled on the floor, and he stepped out of them, leaving his lanky frame nude. She couldn't stop herself from touching him. Her fingers explored his furry thighs before they wrapped around the base of his shaft, stroking him the few times it took to transform his cock from semi-hard to steely.

Morgan rubbed the head of his erection across her lips, then licked the slippery fluid from them while staring up into Joe's eyes.

Could he read her devotion in the artless stare?

"Enough, I'd like to last more than three minutes."

She grinned. "I'm sure you can hold out for five at least. Just give me a taste."

Joe's hands cupped her face and guided her toward his cock. She parted her lips.

Drawing him inside, she traced every line and ridge of his shaft with the tip of her tongue. When she hit the spot on the underside that drove him bananas, he growled.

Joe reached beneath her arms to lift her. She hitched one thigh over his hip. He boosted her with a palm on her ass, allowing her to wrap her other leg tight around his waist. They made out while the water warmed.

After minutes of foreplay more delicious than the chocolate mousse cake she'd baked last week, steam billowed around them. She leaned back a bit to flick the buttons of Joe's borrowed shirt open one at a time, revealing herself to him inch by inch. Never before had she had so much self-confidence in her figure.

The hunger in his eyes never lied, though. He craved her as much as she did him. Something she would never stop being thankful for.

She tossed the well-worn flannel into the white wicker hamper. No need for that with him around to keep her toasty.

They groaned in unison when their bare chests met.

Joe shimmied against her, teasing her breasts with his pecs. As if he knew it would leave her breathless, he repeated the sinuous caress before she could beg for more. All the while his cock prodded her clit, poising her on the verge of climax before they'd truly gotten started.

They didn't pause their slow grind when he stepped into the enclosure. Gentle trickles from the rain shower showerhead cascaded over them.

Ever thoughtful, he angled the spray against the tile for a bit before pressing her to the heated surface. "I know I had you earlier, but I swear I'm about to explode all over you."

"I thought the idea was to come inside me. Again and again." She nipped his neck. "I'm no expert at this baby-making stuff, but I'm pretty sure that's how it works."

"Wench." He ripped the toilet paper from his hand and tossed it toward the trash. The slap he landed on the side of her wet ass with his now-bare palm reverberated off the tile surround.

"Come on, Joe." She wriggled, attempting to notch his cock in the opening of her pussy. "Fuck me."

Joe pinned her with his shoulders so he could wedge his hand between them. Pressing his cock down with two fingers on top of the shaft, he aimed the swollen purple head between her thighs. Slippery. He glided through her slit, coating himself with her arousal. Every pass poked her clit with the blunt cap of his erection.

She shivered.

"You're ready." He murmured into her neck, licking and nipping as he pressed against her, letting gravity do some of the work. She slid down, hugging the first couple inches of his cock even as he stretched her. No matter how many times they did this, he altered her, forcing her body to accommodate his.

"Always ready for you." She tipped her head back until her crown *thunked* against the tile and soothing drizzle misted her face.

Joe screwed deeper within her, each twitch of his hips merging them together more completely. Never once did she worry he might drop her. "You're so hot. Burning me. So sweet."

He sucked on her chin, then migrated to her mouth where he toyed with her tongue while he embedded himself completely. She hung, impaled on his shaft, rocking in order to rub the ache in her clit on the hard muscles above the base of his cock. He started to move inside her with nearly as much urgency as she felt. His balls tapped her ass when he really got going.

Counterparts—she took when he gave, and gave when he took.

Each round-trip of his taxiing cock had her channel tightening further. Soon, Joe could hardly move within her as every inch of her tissue clung to him, squeezing him. Undulations began at her core, sucking him in despite his attempts to retreat if only to slam home once more.

"Damn. Love it when you do that." He cupped her breasts, soothing the pressure caused by her diamond-tipped nipples. "More."

"Not voluntary. Happens when you fuck me just right." She realized her eyes had slid closed as she reveled in bliss. The lack of visual stimulation only encouraged her brain to detect other pleasurable sensations.

"Like this?" He swiveled his hips in a sinful figure eight.

"Yes!" She no longer felt the water on her face or the slight chill creeping in around the edge of the shower curtain. The only thing that mattered was bonding with her mate and maybe creating something new and wondrous, half her and half him.

The idea held so much appeal she unraveled in his arms.

She mouthed Joe's name, but couldn't hear any sound beyond the rush of blood in her veins and the pounding of her heart—so close to his. Strung tight, she arched in his rock-solid grip. Her heels drummed on his ass as rounds of spasms wracked her. She couldn't breathe, couldn't move, couldn't tell this man how much she adored him. Except by opening her eyes and putting her soul on display for him to read.

Joe stared straight into her eyes. Message received. He smiled and dropped his forehead to hers, allowing himself to fray around the edges. He rammed into her harder than he would consider appropriate when not at the height of passion. She loved every second.

He shouted, a guttural cry filled with jumbled babble that her heart translated into perfect sense.

Heat spread through her abdomen—whether she imagined it or she could really sense it remained a mystery. She cheered every grunt that accompanied a pulse of his cock and the resulting mess he made of her pussy.

Good luck, boys. She giggled when she realized she cheered on a bunch of sperm.

"What's...funny?" Joe didn't look nearly as amused. He panted between bites and kisses on her neck and shoulders. "Laughing because I didn't give you a dozen orgasms before I lost it? Give me a minute and I'll make it up to you."

"Not that at all." She worked his cock with her pussy, using the tricks Kayla had taught her and the rest of the crew women, even as Joe set her feet carefully on the tub floor without separating them. Erotic massage techniques came in handy, who knew?

Joe's eyes rolled back. "Jesus. That should be illegal. Wicked."

"I told you Kay is a bad influence."

"Pretty sure I like you corrupted." He groaned when she paused then flexed again. His legs trembled. She stood on her tiptoes, not willing to break the connection of their bodies just yet.

"I'm not ready to get out." No surprise, he articulated her thoughts. He held her hand to keep her from leaving, as if she would consider that option in a million years. "Stay in here. Where the world is made up of you and me. You're the only thing that matters."

He sank to the floor of the basin, sprawling on his back in the garden tub, another upgrade he'd insisted on undertaking for her. She could fully appreciate the benefits of his hard work.

"No, you are." Morgan followed him down. She cuddled against his humid skin, lapping at the nearest droplets dotting its surface. His salty flavor tasted like perfection to her. If only she could use him as the secret ingredient in her culinary creations, she'd be unstoppable.

They petted each other, touched, explored and soothed. It must have been a while because Morgan began to shiver despite their proximity and the still-warm spray spritzing them. The backup water heater he'd installed when she'd started serving customers in the bakery marked another point in his favor. She whimpered when Joe shifted, reluctant to end their snuggle session.

"Don't worry, I'm still not going anywhere." He leaned forward far enough to flip the drain closed and switch the water flow to the gorgeous new spigot he'd installed earlier. With one arm slung around her shoulders, he pumped some bubble bath beneath the stream, filling the tub. He grabbed a lighter and ignited the wick on the candle she kept on the surround for the nights she indulged in a proper soak while reading. She adored Sweet Treats, but being on her feet all day made the decadence part necessity.

"What would the crew think if they saw you taking a bubble bath?" Morgan licked his collarbone. Her hand wandered across his chest and down his washboard abs. His softened cock had long ago slipped from her. Half-hard, it bobbed with the rising tide.

Warmth suffused her as their bodies were submerged.

"They'd think I'm a lucky bastard to be sharing it with you." He nuzzled her temple. "Especially once I get laid again."

"Awful sure of yourself, aren't you?"

"Am I wrong?"

"Hell, no." Morgan straddled his thighs. She gathered huge handfuls of the growing foam and spread it all over her chest and belly.

Joe cursed and reached for her.

She smacked his hands. "Put them on the sides of the tub and leave them there."

He complied, gritting his teeth all the while. "For how long?"

"Until I say so." She peeked at his fingers. They turned white from gripping the edge of the tub and the handle of the built-in soap dish on the other side. The corner of her mouth tipped up in an evil grin. "Remember when Kay gave us that nuru massage demonstration?"

"God, yes," he hissed.

"I've been thinking about asking her for some lessons." Morgan glopped more bubbles onto Joe's chest, then slithered across his frame. When she slid lower, she used her feet on the front wall of the tub to propel herself up his body once more.

"If we're not careful, I'm going to drown." He gurgled when her breasts and mound rubbed along his entire front.

"Imagine how much slipperier that seaweed goop is." She repeated her circuit, loving the contact of all his severe angles with her lush curves.

"Might make you too hard to hold on to." He grabbed her ass, spreading her cheeks as he tugged her where he wanted her. She rotated her hips to stroke his rejuvenated hard-on, trapped between them.

"I'm not trying to escape. Promise." She put her hands on his shoulders and boosted herself six inches higher. "But since you were bad and moved your hands, I think you should make it up to me by giving me your cock."

His cheeks flushed before her eyes. "I love it when you talk dirty."

"Really?" She lifted her brows. "Like when I say I need you to open me up and push your thick shaft inside my dripping pussy? Or when I say, I can't wait to feel you pumping your load inside me again, filling me with your come...?"

"Jesus. Yes. That." He shattered her illusion of control by plunging into her from below.

Thank God. She relaxed her thighs, allowing him to inhabit her fully. This time they had a tiny bit more restraint. They rippled together, gently for the most part, though surges punctuated the peace and tranquility of their joining.

She gave up attempting to articulate everything in her soul and relied on her body to speak his language. If his answering moans and caresses were any indication, he understood perfectly.

Their tender sharing escalated into something tinged with desperation and longing. Neither of them noticed the water and thick foam sloshing onto the floor. They wouldn't have cared if they had.

The waves they generated facilitated their rhythm, buffeting them and rocking them together with prurient insistence. Morgan bit her lip, hard.

"It's okay," Joe murmured. "There's plenty more of this. Come, Morgan. Never hold back. I'll always provide you as much as you need."

Her body obeyed his mastery. Nails sank into his biceps as she came around him. He never flinched from her full-on display of passion. Instead, he pressed into her with long, strong glides that extended her pleasure until she nearly forgot her own name.

Only when the contractions lessened did he shout and release within her.

The rough seas they'd inspired calmed to a steady lap of waves that shook them both in the wake of their spent passion. Morgan sighed as they threatened to rock her to sleep. Probably not a great idea while still in the tub.

"Time for bed." Joe stifled a yawn. He flipped the drain with his foot, nodding when the valve opened smoothly even after the alterations he'd made.

"Already?" Despite the lassitude permeating her bones, it couldn't be past seven o'clock. "I just got up."

"I didn't say sleep." Joe grinned.

"Seriously? What were they feeding you up North?" She tried not to wince, imagining him invading her swollen pussy again so soon.

"Hey, I didn't say fool around either." He clutched her to him as he rose. Water sluiced from his cut frame. "I missed you. I'd like to catch up. Tell me how your weekend was. Did you try that new recipe I copied from my Aunt

Bianca? She was thrilled and flattered you might use it."

"Oh! Yeah, it was as good as you remembered. Better than you said, even." Morgan poured out a detailed recounting of the tests she'd conducted to improve the balance of flavors.

Joe's stomach growled.

"Want me to run downstairs and check the fridge for leftovers?" She patted his flat belly.

"Nah. I'm sure I'll have a slice or five tomorrow." Joe relinquished her to stand on her own long enough to towel off. He plucked her from the bathmat and carried her to their bed the instant she'd finished.

They burrowed under the covers together, exchanging stories and news. She shook her head at the antics of his Carter cousins. Together with the crew, the six guys—a collection of lost souls Joe's uncle had adopted after the untimely death of his wife—were rowdy enough to stir up trouble even in the middle of nowhere.

Eventually, they'd shared the peaceful evening together—though the time flew by—complete with a couple pieces of cold pizza and the remainder of her test creations, which Joe had inhaled, unable to restrain himself. A tough job, but someone had to do it. Having the foundation for her happiness nearby cleared her mind. She made her decision in a snap after debating all weekend.

"I'm going to tell the girls as soon as I have the chance." Morgan was grateful he nodded without her having to elaborate. She should have realized he'd be on the same page even hours later. It made it easier for her to continue, though she had to clear her throat before she could force the rest out. "They'll need to know to understand why I'm going to wear a diaphragm and insist on condoms next time we're together. The whole group, I mean."

"But—" Joe's jaw slackened. "Are you saying? What happened with James this morning? More of that? *Beyond* that?"

"Yeah, we discussed it and we'd like to try swapping." She wondered if he would love or hate the idea. "How do you feel about that?"

"Wow." He sank deeper into the pile of pillows. "You all *were* busy while we were gone."

"And..."

"Most of me says *hell yeah*." He scrubbed his hand through his not-quite-dry hair. "And part of me is unsure."

"Which part is which?" Morgan draped over his chest, relishing the strength of his arms, which came around her instantly.

"I think it would be smoking hot to watch the rest of the crew spoil you." He licked an imaginary crumb from her neck. "I'll never forget your birthday. I still remember how sweet that cake tasted when we all ate it off you."

She would cherish the memory until the day she died.

"But...you know...the other girls." He rubbed the back of his neck.

"Having sex with them?" she supplied, adoring his stumble considering the libertine delights she'd witnessed him and his friends indulge in.

"Yeah. That's a big step. Huge. You're like sisters. I couldn't stand it if we fucked that up." He sighed. "It took a while for the crew to find our balance with each other. It's not easy when all those connections linger. They can glue you together or trip you up. What if everyone gets tangled into a giant knot?"

"You've already been with Kate," she reminded him gently.

"True. But that was before you."

"I appreciate what you're saying. It's those worries exactly that made me hesitate. Still, I feel like we already have these crazy bonds. Do you really think we could ever drift apart?" They both considered in silence for a few moments.

"No." He reached the same conclusion she had after she'd mulled it over. "We're one unit now. With that said, if something starts to happen and you decide it's not what you thought, or it makes you uncomfortable—"

"What if it turns me on to think of you with them?" She squirmed enough to admit exactly which part of her liked the proposition.

"Is that a hypothetical question?" He looked at her as if afraid this was some kind of sick trap.

"I'm willing to try just about anything once." She nibbled her bottom lip. "And I can think of a lot of things that would be lower on my list. We're so close. It feels unnatural to limit ourselves."

"My guess is the rest of the crew would agree with you. I do." Joe threaded their fingers together. "I would bet my share of the business that we're not the only ones having this discussion tonight either."

"I know how much I respect and love the other guys. I believe that goes both ways."

"Is that a bisexual crack?" He smirked, diffusing some of the tension simmering between them.

"No, but it would have been one hell of a that's-what-*he*-said joke if Kay were here to seize the opportunity." Morgan shook her head, clearing the distraction. "What I'm saying is this... Why would I want you or any of our circle of friends to have roadblocks to expressing our affection for each other?"

"How in the hell did I get so lucky?" Joe rolled, flipping her onto her back. He smothered her so well she wished she never had to draw another breath. "I have the best friends a guy could ask for. A sexy, sweet and dirty wife. And a collection of equally awesome women who all hope to get it on with me."

Morgan laughed. "That's a guy's perspective for sure, but... I suppose you do have it pretty damn good."

"And I'll never forget it." He lowered his face, bringing his lips down on hers, and blanketing her with his flaring heat. "I swear to you. I will always cherish you. And the crew. Our family. However big, small or unconventional."

With that, they *practiced* the whole night long.

CHAPTER FIVE

Devon tucked a flat pencil behind her ear. She hauled the marked crown-molding to the compound miter saw in the corner, then flipped her safety glasses into place. The whir of the blade never ceased to impress and thrill her. In the blink of an eye, the long piece became two smaller ones.

Building something polished from raw materials, transforming an ordinary space into a home that met its full potential, had satisfied her since she first visited a job site with Ray. Her older half-brother, her mother's son from her first marriage, was a mason. He'd allowed her to wander freely between the various contractors as long as she kept out of his hair. Babysitting had never been his forte. At the end of the day, he'd found her crouched beside the foreman, who flipped through pictures of the house they worked on in various stages of its construction.

She'd discovered her professional passion when she was twelve years old. The fascination had grown over the past decade. But the crew elevated her craft to new levels. Though she'd been around the business forever, nothing had rivaled their attention to detail, flair for design or pride in their workmanship. Each man was held in high regard in his area of specialty. The friendship they shared enhanced their partnership. And now that dream team miraculously included her on its roster.

She grinned and bopped to Hot Chelle Rae's "Tonight, Tonight". The party anthem blasted through the beat-up radio they toted from site to site. It might rely on duct tape to hold it together, but it kept her entertained. Her shimmy punctuated the chorus. Dancing on the Hollywood sign couldn't match the euphoria her career and partners produced.

After checking the alignment of the angle, she dry-fitted the pieces on the ground before climbing her ladder to shoot a couple brads into the detail. With the finishing touches on the dining room as complete as she could make them, she hopped down to the hardwood floor, hands on hips, and surveyed the fruits of her labor. Pretty damn fine if she said so herself.

Devon rotated her wrists, which ached a bit from the awkward angle she'd had them at most of the morning. She peered through the plastic sheeting intended to confine dust to her workspace, into the living room. This house would make a great starter home for someone, complete with a smattering of furniture even.

Some of the pieces abandoned by the former residents, who'd moved suddenly following a job offer out of state, had great character. Devon planned to beg Kate to undertake some experimental reupholstering of Neil's hideous college-days sofa so she could apply the learning to sprucing up this set. She could picture the finished product in her mind.

Plus, it would be a handy skill, allowing her to bring something new and different to the crew's capabilities. Win-win, it would also eliminate the burnt sienna plaid monstrosity from her home. Their home. James would definitely vote in her favor on this one.

A rustle from behind her had her glancing over her shoulder.

"Came to lend a hand. Doesn't look like you need our assistance, though." Neil ambled into the room with the rest of the guys in tow.

Dust clung to their holey jeans and T-shirts. Dirt streaked their arms. Exertion had their cheeks glowing. Rugged and filthy, they still managed to steal her breath. Maybe more than when they spruced themselves up.

They'd focused on demolition and the structural concerns rampant in the basement while she completed the more refined project on the main level. Worked for her, except she'd missed having them nearby. Okay, so one stinking floor below her didn't constitute a huge rift. Still, it was enough. Anywhere beyond her grasp seemed too far.

Their faith in her skills overwhelmed her with smugness. They wouldn't allow her to roam unbridled if they had any doubt about her capabilities.

Mike inspected her progress carefully. "This is good shit, Dev. I like how you built up the molding with the dental piece on top of the cove. Looks fantastic. Cost effective. Solid workmanship too. It's stuff like this buyers will notice and pay more for. They don't give a crap that we've made sure their foundation won't crack and sprayed enough insulation in this place to save them a boatload on energy bills. Nice work."

"Thanks, *boss*." She giggled when he smacked her ass with one of his leather gloves. She couldn't resist teasing. "Was that my reward?"

"Careful or I'll put you over my knee, imp." Mike's warning held no heat, unless it was the kind borne of desire.

"Promise?" She would have liked to play more. If there wasn't one last thing she had to attend to. "Seriously, though, I couldn't reach the tray section, even with the ladder. Could one of you hammer this in for me?"

The twitch of Neil's lips guaranteed he'd caught her double entendre. "I suppose I could toss it a couple bangs, since I have such a big tool."

"Have a big tool or *are* a big tool?" Dave smirked.

"That's what *he* said," Devon said simultaneously. She groaned when none of the crew laughed along with her.

Mike imitated a sad trombone with a descending *waa waa waa*.

At least they didn't have any rotten tomatoes or rubber chickens on hand. Suddenly she had a lot more sympathy for Fozzie Bear. Devon stuck out her lower lip. "Aw, party poopers."

"Dave, you have to wrestle Kay under control." Joe smacked their friend in the gut with his knuckles. "She's got all of our girls doing it now."

"That's what *he* said," James quipped and high-fived Devon.

"I knew I loved you for a reason." She stole a kiss, aching for more than the tiny nibble. She hoped he understood how much she adored his infallible instincts, which ensured she was never the odd "man" out.

"Yeah, and let Kayla hear you talk about muffling her. She'll rip you a new one. Or better yet, maybe she'll tattle on you to Morgan." Mike shook his head.

"Oh please, no." Joe held his index fingers out in a cross as though warding off a clan of vampires on the attack. "I promise. I'll be good."

Devon's face hurt from smiling so huge, caught in the crossfire of their banter. She loved them so much tears pricked her eyes. Quickly, she put her back to the crew and shoved her safety glasses on top of her head like the least designer headband of all time. Kneeling as though tidying her workspace, she scrubbed surreptitiously at her cheeks.

James crouched by her side. His hand rubbed a soothing arc across her back. "What did we say?"

Only then did she realize the room had gone silent, her playlist complete.

She dropped her head on his shoulder and rooted her face into his neck. "You didn't do anything wrong."

"What's all this?" Neil bracketed her. With one hand on James's shoulder, he nudged her chin up so he could peer at her face.

"I can't believe how lucky I am." She sniffled. "Dumb, I know. But you make me so happy. Sometimes I'm afraid I'm dreaming and that I'll wake up and you'll all be gone. A figment of my imagination."

"That's kind of fucked up, Dev," Joe murmured from behind her where he, Dave and Mike stood shoulder to shoulder, guarding her back.

"Gee, thanks." She snorted. "Okay, now I know you're real men."

"We're in this for the long haul." Mike dropped a hand to her stubby ponytail and mussed the strands already flying free, since her hair was really too short for the 'do.

"You couldn't get rid of us if you tried." Dave towered over her. His commanding presence reassured her. They all did.

She reached out to Neil and James. Neil nibbled on her trembling fingers, layering kisses along the digits he cradled as delicately as if they were a precisely calibrated set of calipers. He paid special attention to her ring finger and the stylized tattoo gracing it. They'd offered to buy her a ring. Fought with her over it, actually, until she convinced them the extravagance would go to waste. Safety prohibited her from wearing jewelry most of the time.

Truth be told, she preferred the indelible marking—a vine that wound around the base of her finger and cradled two flowers that mimicked center stones, one red and one yellow, the guys' favorite colors—as permanent as their residency in her heart. If the artwork bore traces of sawdust, Neil didn't seem to mind. More like his breath steamed harder against her wrist when his tongue traced the proof of their possession.

James captured her mouth. He coaxed her lips apart with skill and finesse that never ceased to amaze her. For a guy who claimed to prefer men most of the time, he sure as hell knew how to trip every single one of her passionate triggers.

He dazzled her with the thrill he inspired. Dizzy, she tipped into Neil's waiting embrace. He rose smoothly to his feet, lifting her too.

"Come here." He must have aimed the directive at James, because she had no choice except to go where he toted her. Not that she minded. Never would she have complained.

His gruff commands echoed through the space, which they'd cleared furniture from.

Devon closed her eyes as Neil ducked beneath the plastic shield they'd hung in the arched opening to the living room. When Mike, Dave and Joe evaluated his trajectory and guessed where Neil intended to place her, they jogged ahead.

Mike ripped the protective sheet from the worn leather couch and stripped the seat cushions off. He tossed one to Joe and another to Dave. Between the three of them, they converted the rustic coffee table into a padded dais faster than James's adopted kitty invaded the kitchen when he heard his savior rustling a bag of pricey organic kibble. Only the best for everything and everyone James loved.

Spoiled rotten and reveling in it, Devon winked up at the crew.

Neil swooped in to kiss her even as her legs were tugged from his grip. Her safety glasses clattered to the ground, skidding somewhere under the chair. Devon gasped when someone, James if the deft yet caressing hands were any indication, unclasped her tool belt, unlaced and disposed of her boots, then swiped her jeans off in no time flat. She wobbled on shaky legs when they shifted their attention to stripping her top half.

Thank God for the electric heaters they'd installed to keep the house cozy. They hadn't overhauled the plumbing yet and wouldn't take a chance on a busted pipe until they had.

She gulped for air like a fish out of water once her mouth ripped free of Neil's, their connection severed by the passing of her thermal top. One of the guys nudged her arms up while another whipped the cotton from her body. Left in her cute yet utilitarian cotton bra and panties, she didn't feel the least bit exposed.

"Your underwear is yellow." Neil traced the skin beside the cheery straps.

"With red hearts." James nipped at one cartoony symbol gracing the curve of her hip.

"What better to hug my lady parts all day than something that reminds me of you two?" Her whisper carried in the hush of the calm before the storm.

"*Nothing* would be pretty damn fine. Imagining you naked beneath those funky, patched overalls you wear sometimes gives me massive wood." Neil grimaced when several of them paused to consider that mental image. Dave cursed under his breath.

She laughed out loud. Too bad she hadn't known that before their Valentine's Day photo session. Although she doubted there'd be any complaints when he discovered the Victorian getup she'd stashed in the back of their closet. It *had* made her waist look tiny.

"What?" Neil shrugged. "I have to have something extra special to daydream about when I'm stuck worming around in dark, dingy crawlspaces to examine foundations, or evaluate attics, or check for mold, or whatever other duties these guys claim the skinniest of us should be on the hook for. If I thought about rats or spiders or asbestos monsters lurking in those tight spots, I'd flip out."

Devon laid her hand on his forearm. "I'll take inspection duty next time. You shouldn't have to if it makes you uncomfortable. I'm the littlest. Not afraid of bugs either. And claustrophobia has never been an issue. I kind of like being crowded."

As if by tacit understanding, each crew member took a step closer. Their heat and hunger blasted her from all sides as they encroached on her personal space. She closed her eyes and leaned toward Neil, trusting him to catch her.

Of course, he did. They guided her to the improvised bed they'd constructed. She yelped at the initial contact of the cool leather on her skin. Ten hands petted and soothed her until they abolished any hint of chill.

"Scoot over, Dev." James whipped his clothes off, then nudged her hip with his knee. She made room for him to join her. "I'm in the mood to share the bottom with you today."

"Or do you mean share *your* bottom?" She nipped his lip when he slipped his arm beneath her neck, supporting her.

"Either works for me." He pressed a delicate peck on the tip of her nose. "But I wouldn't dare steal your fun."

"There's plenty to go around." She switched her gaze from man to man to man to man, ringing them.

When she licked her lips, they shed chambray, denim and leather as if it were a race. Maybe it was. Dave finished first. Though Devon expected him to reach for James, or maybe the industrial-sized bottle of lube they kept in their tool chest, he didn't. Instead, he straddled the head of the coffee table, planting one foot on either side of her and James. He squatted until his thick cock hung between their faces.

"Ladies first." James rolled onto his side, and she mirrored him.

Devon reached upward to fondle the heavy sac swaying gently in the aftermath of Dave's gymnastics. It still felt new and somewhat taboo to be touching Kayla's husband. A thrill zinged through her, accompanied by a shiver that vibrated along her spine. The tremble had her hand retracting, severing her contact with Dave's electrified skin.

Did this adhere to their slumber party agreement? Or was she crossing the boundaries by indulging without her girlfriends?

She tried to work out the intricacies in her lust-hazed mind without much success. All she could say for sure was that her visceral response to the situation instilled a craving, the intensity of which she'd never known before. Or at least not since the first time she'd had James and Neil together.

"Trust your instincts." James came to her rescue. "He likes it like this."

He demonstrated a firmer grip than Dev would have been comfortable imparting on her own.

"Go ahead." Dave barked instructions. "Do me like he's showing you. It feels fucking great."

She hesitated, her hand a fraction of an inch away from her goal.

"Am I allowed to?" She hated the pale imitation of her voice. "I've never…"

"Kay confessed to me about your scheming the other night." He growled. "Time to put your mouth where your fantasies are. If you still want this. Me. Us."

The note of uncertainty in his gruff admission had Devon reaching out in a flash. Her insecurities would never affect the rest of the crew if she had anything to say about it.

He gasped and might have toppled if James hadn't braced the bigger man's bulging thigh. Devon didn't blink twice. They'd never allow her to be crushed. She focused on her prize, cupping his nuts in her palm. The heavy sac covered in soft skin nestled into her palm.

James lectured her on refining her technique. He offered subtle adjustments to her clutch. When she had Dave panting and groaning softly, they moved to phase two of their tandem attack.

Devon grinned across at James. He smacked his lips together while staring at the damp head of Dave's cock.

"There's enough to share," she whispered. "Probably can't fit him all in my mouth anyway. Suck him with me, James."

She twined her fingers in the neat strands of her mate's hair and used the clutch to coax him nearer. Not that he resisted much. When his tongue flicked from between his lips, she mimicked his technique. Together, they laved every inch of Dave's shaft from the base to just below the head. Veins grew in definition beneath each timid lap of her tongue.

From time to time, James would get carried away. His lips clashed with hers around the cylinder of Dave's cock. She gasped. Dave took advantage of the situation to poke his hard-on into her mouth. His girth stretched her lips into a wide O.

James traced the semi-circle closest to him with the tip of his tongue.

"Jesus. That's sexy, Dev." Neil leaned in to kiss her cheek. Although he had serviced James on special occasions more recently, it was a true act of love for him. He didn't derive pleasure from giving blowjobs. The crew respected his limits. Knowing his face lingered so near his friend's cock had Devon whimpering.

The vibration must have done wonderful things to Dave's shaft because the big man sighed and sank lower, feeding her more of his cock.

James took advantage of the opportunity. He stretched his neck upward and engulfed Dave's balls. He sucked first one, then the other. The wet slurps and smacks inspired her to draw a few more inches of their friend inside her.

"Give me a break," Dave groaned. "Or I'm gonna shoot before we've really gotten started."

Devon giggled around his beast of a cock.

Neil cupped her cheeks in his palms and drew her off his friend's length. James rejoined her, abandoning his oral massage of the sensitive tissues between Dave's thighs.

He tossed her a devilish grin, then nipped at Neil's restraining fingers.

"Ouch. That stung, asshole." Neil let go and shook his hand. His rebuke was hard to take seriously when he laughed through his curses.

"Just remember payback is a bitch." Mike slapped James's bare ass from his spot behind their lover. The crack reverberated off the hardwood floors gracing their latest project.

"Yeah. Except I fucking love that, you bastard." James hooked an arm around Devon's waist and tugged until their pelvises ground together. His erection never failed to impress her with its ultra-hardness. Though the rest of the guys had him in length and girth, he had more than enough to please her. After all, it was less about the tool and more about his proficiency in handling it.

James had skills beyond belief.

They bumped together until Devon was sure her panties had soaked through. Why wouldn't someone touch her?

"Is this what you want, little one?" Joe flicked his fingers over the catch of her bra. The pressure of the straps on her shoulders made it clear he planned to divest her of the extra-padded push-up. She lifted her arms, careful not to whack Dave in the family jewels. She might not have a lot to warrant the garment, but she was vain enough to enhance what little she had. Hopefully the guys didn't see it as false advertising. She'd never be as stacked as Kate or Morgan.

She shouldn't have worried.

Joe knelt on the floor behind her, cupping her chest in his calloused palms. The slight abrasion launched shafts of pleasure from her breasts to her pussy.

"Yes," she moaned. "More."

Neil released her, dragging his hands along the stretched column of her neck. He outlined the hold Joe had on her, making both of the guys' respiration grow ragged. Joe shifted his fingers to blanket Neil's for an instant before they continued their trek toward her belly. Neil paused to span her waist, as he often did. Both of them enjoyed how large he was compared to her diminutive form.

She lifted up when his hands tucked into the waistband of her panties. He peeled them from her so fast she was relieved she didn't get some kind of friction burn. At least he hadn't shredded this pair. She was rather fond of them. More so after today.

They cleared her matching red-painted toes, a remnant of the weekend photo shoot. He sling-shotted them at Mike. They all stared as the foreman brought the cotton to his face and breathed deep, like an alpha wolf memorizing the scent of a member of his pack.

"Sweet." He dropped the scrap of fabric onto the pile of clothes littering the floor. "Will you let me taste you too?"

Devon glanced between Neil and James. Neither of them objected. She squeaked when James reached down to hoist her knee toward her chest, opening her to their crewmates. "He's really good with his mouth, Dev. You don't want to miss out."

And there it was.

The truth. She didn't want to miss out anymore. This tension had zinged through them for months now. Every time the crew expressed their affection and relieved some stress on the job site, she cooled her heels on the sidelines. Granted, she already felt like she had an unfair advantage over some of the crew wives for her ringside seat to those glorious shows, but she'd longed to cross their unspoken boundaries and truly become one of the crew.

Today, there would be no stopping short. No embargos placed on the pure adoration in her heart. These men were hers and she was theirs. Though not many others would understand, she thanked the universe every single day that she'd found the family she'd never really had but always needed so desperately.

"Yes. Please, Mike." She would never forget the glitter in his eyes as he descended on her. It came close to the fire in her soul for the man who'd glued them all together.

The moment his lips brushed her core, she wilted, surrendering to his authority, which ordered her to relax and accept his gift. Once her eyes had stopped rolling back at the initial onslaught of pleasure, she realized Dave had cradled her head, granting her a clear view of Mike as he peppered her waxed mound with light, feathery kisses.

"So smooth," he rumbled against her sensitive flesh.

"Benefit of having a friend who owns a spa." She managed to force out the revelation between gritted teeth.

"Another reason I love my wife." Dave sighed dreamily. His cock lurched, rising up to paint a sticky trail across Devon's cheek with the dripping head. "I can't wait to tell her about this. She'll go crazy, begging me to fuck her, imagining she was the one to taste you. You know she wants that. Bad. Don't you, Dev? She cares for you. She'll be so happy you finally got what you've wanted."

When he put it so simply, Devon's lingering guilt evaporated. It would be impossible to deny the honesty of his rambling when desire acted like a truth serum, causing him to blurt out the deepest secrets in his heart.

"I dream about it too, Dave." She angled her head to kiss along the side of his thick shaft. James echoed her motion. They sandwiched Dave's cock between their hot, moist mouths, licking, sucking and sliding up and down his length again. Their dual blowjob was sloppy, but he didn't seem to mind. Some of his control restored, he helped them by rocking into their grip, fucking their faces relentlessly as Mike continued his reverent exploration.

"Damn, that's sexy." Joe stroked her back from his place behind her. "You're a natural, Dev. I always wondered what it'd be like to have shared you with the crew. Each of our girls is so different. Being with Kate the first time... Shit. I'll never forget that scorching afternoon. And seeing how much these guys could please Morgan, I would never deny her that. You either. I hope we can make it half as good for you."

While he continued his generous speech, he caressed her from head to toe. Neil moved out of his way, circling around the table to stand behind James instead. Joe stroked her hair, rubbed her shoulders and took over for

James, supporting her knee so Mike had clear access to her pussy. James used his newly freed hand to reach behind him and connect with Neil. He didn't have to look to find their mate.

"Yeah," Neil groaned. "Go with it. Both of you."

Devon's lashes fluttered as she struggled to keep them open. She made direct eye contact with James. His gorgeous eyes seared a stare into hers and she knew she'd never feel lonely again. Not with him and the rest of these men surrounding her. His pupils dilated, and he gasped around Dave's shaft before releasing the plaintive whimper she'd come to associate with the initial burn of someone penetrating his ass.

She abandoned Dave's cock to soothe James instead. Distracting him with open-mouthed kisses, she helped him relax enough to accept the lubed fingers Neil surely worked into his ass.

"That's right, James," Neil whispered against James's neck. "Soon you'll have all of me. That's what you needed, isn't it?"

"Yes." He groaned when Neil massaged him from the inside out.

"And you, sweetheart?" Mike lifted his mouth from her long enough to ask. "What would you like?"

"Don't stop." She squirmed until her pussy aligned with his lips again. That talented, deceptively gentle mouth descended.

His chuckles buffeted her nerves. This time, he enhanced the sensation with his fingers. The pressure caused by two of his thick, blunt digits prodding at her entrance had her seeking James's hand.

"Holy shit." Mike paused the figure eight of his tongue to glare at Neil. "Why didn't you warn me? I might have hurt her, rushed her."

"We told you she was tight," they muttered together.

"She's tiny." He sighed and folded one of his fingers against his palm, leaving only his index finger to penetrate her rippling channel.

No matter how she tried to relax, his decadent fondling had her tensed again in no time. "S-sorry."

"Shh. Only worried about causing you pain or frightening you away," Mike murmured against her mound. "Now that I've tasted you, I don't think I could be satisfied with a single serving."

"Want you inside me. Just do it. I don't mind." Her urging turned breathless when he lodged in her to the second knuckle.

"Not concerned about my fingers, cutie." He smiled against her mound. "More afraid of how you'll take my cock. I'm thicker than your guys. And Dave... Well, you might have to work up to him."

Joe groaned from behind her. She didn't like leaving him out of their circle. Devon squirmed, trying to roll over. Mike lifted his head, surveying her predicament.

"Good idea, Dev." The foreman flipped her as if she weighed nothing.

Lying on her back, she was able to wrap her fingers around Joe's shaft. She tugged several times, experimentally. A bead of pre-come dripped from the tip onto her forearm.

"Let me taste that." James drew her arm toward his mouth. He lapped at the slick streak there, making them all groan in appreciation. The wet heat on her skin had a shudder traveling down her body.

Mike cursed when she spasmed around his embedded fingers. When had he fit the other inside her? He scissored them, spreading her tissues gently. "I can't wait for you to hug my dick like that."

Devon whimpered. "Me either."

Joe caught her attention as he stroked himself, unable to wait for gratification. She winced. It would take some practice to service five men at once.

"Don't worry, Dev." Neil grunted. "It's up to us to find our own pleasure. You lay back and enjoy. Let them use you and the rest is our job, okay?"

She nodded.

"Fuck, that's hot." He stared between her thighs where Mike conditioned her pussy even as he nibbled on her lips and around her clit. "James, I need to be inside you."

"Do it." The smaller man huffed when Neil banded his arms around James's waist and used the hold to raise him to his knees.

From her position beside him, it was easy for Devon to reach beneath him and stroke his cock.

"Perfect, Dev." Mike hummed, vibrating her aching flesh. "Slow and easy, just like that. Help him forget about Neil sinking deep."

Devon met Neil's gaze. The cords in his neck stood out as he advanced. James's tight, hot hole must have clamped on his cock. Though they'd done this countless times before, he always had a look of wonder on his face when he mounted his lover. Devon hoped the same could be said for his liaisons with her.

James lifted his head. Breathing hard, his panting buffeted Dave's neatly trimmed pubic hair, which dusted the base of his monster hard-on. James didn't need to be asked. He opened his mouth and reached out with one arm to smack Dave's ass, goading him closer.

"You want it rough today?" Dave seemed eager to comply. He tugged on James's hair, positioning her mate's open mouth at the head of his cock. "I can fuck you as well as Neil can from here."

James's moan was all the encouragement he needed. Dave buried himself to the root in James's mouth. The shorter man choked a little, but held his place. He had nowhere to go, really. Pierced from behind by Neil and pinned in front by Dave, they skewered him.

The throb of his erection in her still-stroking hand reassured her he wouldn't have fled if he could. He'd be more likely to chase them down and beg them to fuck him.

"Shit. That's fucking hot." Joe used one hand to pinch his own nipple as he pulled on his cock with the other.

"Poor Joe." Mike *tsked* against her clit, making her mewl and beg for more. "You're not going to leave him hanging out there all alone, are you?"

Devon didn't have to be told twice. She swiveled her head, and Joe met her halfway. He ringed his erection with his fist at the base, ensuring she didn't attempt to take more than she could handle. She teased his head with flicks of her tongue, like James had taught her, interspersed with strong draws that hollowed her cheeks.

"Oh, Christ." He knelt, or half-folded, so his knees rested on the table beside her. From there he grounded himself with a palm on her breast. "She sucks as well as James."

"Good teacher." Her retort jumbled around the mass of his cock. But they got her point.

Mike admonished her. "Watch your teeth now."

She folded her lips over the sharp edges, although certain she hadn't nicked Joe. Only when the wide cap of Mike's erection prodded her saturated pussy did she realize what he'd meant. She froze as he began to enter her, a fraction of an inch at a time.

"Oh. Fuck." Dave grunted as he shuttled in and out of James's mouth. "You should see this. He's opening her up and she's loving it."

James paused, removing his mouth with a slurp so he could tuck his head between his shoulders and witness Mike's progress for himself. "Are you okay, Dev?"

His wide eyes made her sure it looked as drastic as it felt. The invasion burned, stretched and caressed her in new and wonderful ways she hadn't expected.

"Love it. God, yes." She answered by increasing the pace of her hand, which jerked him with ungraceful passes now that sensations bombarded her from all angles.

Neil helped when he fucked James harder, faster, thrusting James's cock through the ring of her fingers and eliminating the need for her to move at all.

"More, sweetheart?" Mike rode her with short strokes, bumping them together just enough for her to sample what he might really do if he pushed inside her to the hilt.

"All of you." She would have used her heels on his ass to try to force him deeper but she was no match for his strength.

"Not like that." He gritted his teeth. "I won't hurt you. No matter what you think you want, we'll take this slow. Neil, pass me the lube."

She was drenched, plenty slick to take him. Still, she didn't argue when she realized it meant his dexterous fingers would be slipping in and around her pussy beside his gorgeous cock. By thrusting upward, she captured another inch or two of his shaft.

Damn, it did sting. Not more than she could handle. And after a few heartbeats of stillness, the mild pain faded into something a hell of a lot more pleasurable.

"You pay attention here." Joe fed her more of his hard-on. "Let Mike handle that. He's really good at taking someone without hurting them. Especially if they're not used to getting fucked."

Devon glanced up in time to catch the flush spreading across Joe's chest and up his neck. He should know. She'd stared, fascinated, as Joe bent over for their foreman from time to time.

"Jealous?" She pulled off his tip long enough to taunt him.

"Be good or I'll think you don't deserve this treat." He ruffled her hair playfully.

She exacted revenge by relaxing her throat, taking him deeper than ever on the next pass. He traced her lips where they ringed his shaft. She swallowed around him, wriggling her tongue along the underside of his cock.

"Okay, I take it back." He choked. "This is just fine by me."

Devon relented, otherwise she could easily drain his orgasm before they were ready to shatter together. For some reason, it mattered to her. She had to share her climax with the crew in the ultimate wegasm or she wouldn't be satisfied.

"Better speed it up," Dave warned Mike. "She's getting that gleam in her eyes like Kay does when she's ready to rip me apart to have her way. You're not going to hurt her. She wants this. You."

Her stare flicked to Neil's. He read the desperation in her gaze even as he continued to ride their mate. One hand lifted from James's ass to rest on Mike's lower back. He prevented the foreman from retreating and instead, nudged him deeper within her.

Knowing Neil directed the action blew her arousal out of proportion. Logic fled. In its place was only sensation. The smell of men and sex and sweat. The sound of grunts, groans and sighs. The sight of muscles straining, flexing and bulging. The taste of Joe's pre-come, salty and sweet. And the feel…

Oh God, the feel of them.

Over her, under, around, inside… She couldn't help but sense them in every pore of her being. Every breath and heartbeat was filled with the crew.

She had never been happier in her life.

Mike nestled into the cradle of her thighs. Their abdomens met as they fused completely.

"You feel fucking amazing around me." He groaned into her neck as he fell forward for an instant, catching his breath before the sprint to the finish.

Her head lolled onto the cushion as she lost all sense of time and space. Joe's cock slipped from her mouth. Mike picked up her slack. He slurped the thick shaft between his lips, engulfing it in one long stroke.

As he began to move inside her, he fucked Joe with his face, plunging to the base of Joe's erection every time he bottomed out in her pussy. Devon traced the juncture of his lips and Joe's cock while reveling in the glide of Mike's broad, lightly furred chest across her mostly flat torso. They glued together from pelvis to shoulders, one of the few times she didn't mind her lack of endowment.

She pried her stare from the men before her, wanting to check in with her lovers. Her *other* lovers, she supposed. Neil pounded James in the unflinching rhythm they loved best. The smaller man's cock bulged in her grip as though he could sense her teetering on the edge of oblivion.

He met her gaze and smiled around Dave's cock. The tightening of his mouth was the final straw for the burly man. He growled, fisting his hands in James's hair as he slid deep and regular down James's throat.

Devon watched her mate's Adam's apple bob, no doubt wringing every possible drop of pleasure from Dave's cock. The release set off a chain reaction. She stiffened, every part of her—not least of all her mind, heart and soul—affected by the generous affection of the men surrounding her.

The sound that burst from her startled them all, herself included. They froze as they focused on her. The force of their attention guaranteed she'd reached the point of no return. Devon shattered around Mike. She clawed at his back with one hand while the other still clasped James.

Through delirious pleasure, the searing wetness coating her palm and wrist as James shuddered in her hold fueled the fire blazing through her veins. Neil roared, convulsing as he poured himself into James's ass.

Mike whipped his head off Joe's shaft just as the standing crewmate began to grunt and shake. Stream after stream of his ejaculate streaked Devon's chest. She wondered at Mike's choice, since she'd seen him gobble down come enough times to be certain he didn't mind, until he cleaned the evidence of Joe's orgasm from her one rivulet at a time.

Long laps of his tongue accompanied the hammering of his hips. He nailed her with a ferocity counterbalanced by the tenderness of his care. When he skimmed her nipple, she couldn't help but surrender to another climax. Her channel rippled around his cock, sucking semen straight from his balls.

He snarled, then bit her neck. Not enough to hurt. Enough to leave a faint bruise. As he deposited his come deep inside her, none of them could deny he'd staked his claim. As their leader, her mentor and a great friend,

Mike had marked her as belonging to him. Them.

For the first time since she'd joined the crew, she felt fully a part of their unit. The bond she'd shared with her husbands expanded, including all five of the men in the radiance of her affection.

They looked at her, and she stared back. No words were necessary. They all understood. This kind of connection was forever.

What would their wives think of that?

CHAPTER SIX

"**M**organ!" Kate shrieked and dodged the splash of suds from the sink when an earthenware bowl plunged below the surface.

"It was an accident. It slipped in, I swear." She held her wet, soapy hands up in front of her.

"That's what *he* said." Kayla wasn't about to let that one sneak past. She flipped a smirk over her shoulder, but Devon couldn't find the heart to return the cheeky grin.

Instead, she dropped a bomb. "I think I might have cheated on you. All of you."

Kate whipped her apron over her head and came to investigate immediately. She had to have been expecting the meltdown.

Devon wrung her hands in front of her churning guts. She shivered.

"Honey, isn't this kind of déjà vu?" Morgan joined the women where they huddled near the bar, which distinguished Kayla's kitchen from the rest of the open cabin.

"What do you mean?" Dev tipped her head.

"Remember when you came to us as an *intern*?" Kayla laughed. "And P.S., that was total bullshit. You already knew far too much about constructioning for that dumb title."

The fabrication had Devon cracking a smile as her friend had no doubt intended. "Right. I admit it. I lied on my resume by deleting a heck of a lot of experience. But I heard the crew was the best so I took my shot."

"And what happened then?" Kate arched one eyebrow. "The first time you came out here? When you were so afraid we'd hate you for watching the guys touch each other? As if any red-blooded woman could close her eyes to that."

"I didn't think I was so transparent." She scowled.

"Poker faces aren't your strength." Kayla patted her shoulder.

"Yeah well, if I was scared of losing the best thing I'd found in my life then, it's a million times worse now. I know what I'd be sacrificing if I fucked this up." Devon groaned. "They did tell you what happened, right? Please say they did."

"Of course." Kate propped her hand on her hip. It was a little hard to take her glare serious when she was naked. "If it's any consolation, I think Mike was more nervous than you are. I should kick both your asses."

Devon's heart plummeted through the floor. "I earned it."

"For doubting the experience you had? Yes. If it had been wrong, you would have stopped. Any of you. All of you." Kate glared at her. "Did it feel messed up?"

"God no." A wash of residual comfort and homecoming knocked her on her ass on the kitchen stool. "I felt like I belonged."

"You do." Kate hugged her. "Mike told me they claimed you as soon as he burst through the door. Trust me...it takes more than that to satisfy him. If anything, he came home rock hard and ready to play. I think the pressure of the whole baby-making thing freaked him out a bit. It's been a while since I've seen him at the end of his leash like that."

"Honestly, Dev, I had horrible cramps that day." Kayla winced. "You guys did me a pretty big favor. Dave would never pressure me for sex when I'm not feeling good, but I walked in on him jerking off in the shower that morning. I admit it, I tiptoed out of there and he pretended he didn't see me through the steam. I couldn't bring myself to join him right then, and I felt pretty guilty about it until he told me what happened. I like knowing he's being taken care of."

"In that case...I'm glad to help." Devon chuckled when Kayla pinched her arm and called her a tart. "I guess I sort of got overwhelmed, you know? That's not an excuse. I should have thought it through first instead of following my instincts..."

"It's different when they're all together. I remember clearly that day in the pool." Kate's eyes glazed over a bit. "I'll dream about it until the day I die. It's like they're one person. Focused on you. I'd be lying if I said I didn't crave the power of that combined passion. Once Morgan came along, things changed. I'm not sure that was the right decision. Or maybe it was at the time. But we're stronger now. Sure of ourselves and our relationships. We've had time to sort out how our individual partnerships work and how we fit into the group. Maybe we should reevaluate."

"You just want to have them all to yourself again." Kayla winked.

"Maybe someday." Kate's eyes darkened. "I've been thinking about how to make this work. Because the reality is I'd also be lying if I ignored the flash of instinctual jealousy that pricked me when Mike first shared the news he claimed Devon. He told me she was hot, tight and delicate. For a blip, I wondered…would he prefer that all the time? Then he made sure I knew the answer."

"See, I guess I'm hyperaware of the fact that I have a different relationship with the crew." Devon winced. "I mean, I *am* part of them. I work with those assholes every day. I would hate if you thought I was taking advantage of the situation when you're not around. I've enjoyed watching when they would break for a long lunch or when things would heat up on the sites. I think we've been really clear that they'd end up watching me with James and Neil too. But the new touch-if-you-want rule… It changes things. Makes this something more. I just want to be sure that you're sure. Really, really sure. I couldn't stand to screw up what we have, since it's pretty damn amazing already."

Kayla sidled closer, levering herself halfway onto the last free stool at the bar. "The way I see it, you hit the nail on the head there. You *are* one of them. You spend the most time with them. I expect that you have a stronger bond with them. You have so much in common. You're on the border between friend, lover and co-worker. This is going to be harder on you, I think. You have no escape from them. No relief."

"It's true. You have a lot to juggle." Kate laid her hand over Devon's. "But when I start to get confused, I come back to this core truth. Mike's feelings for the crew didn't impact the formation of our love, unless it was to make it stronger. His attachment still doesn't harm our relationship now that our gang has grown beyond the five of them and me. It's the same for your guys and the rest of us."

"I totally agree. But some ground rules probably wouldn't hurt, right?" Morgan asked.

"You've been pretty quiet. What do you think about this?" Kate had clearly spent some time considering the possibilities and come prepared with a plan. "When we're all together, or a whole pair—trio, whatever—is present, it's anything goes as long as the couples involved consent."

"So if Dave and I are hanging out with Neil, James and Dev..." Kayla squinted her eyes as she puzzled through the scenario.

"It's your call." Kate nodded. "There shouldn't be any limits then. But for now, we'll reserve one person bonding with the crew for special occasions. You know, maybe each person's birthday. Sort of like, whoever is celebrating gets to be the centerpiece for the night. They can ask for whatever and whoever they want. No one will be excluded, though. Those not playing could still view if they wanted."

"Damn, who would choose not to?" Kayla shifted in her seat, fanning her rosy cheeks.

"I'm not making anyone else's decisions for them. I feel like if we're in it together, there's nothing seedy about it. When I saw Mike around you at dinner, Dev, I noticed a difference. It felt right to me. He seemed more natural when he interacted with you. He loves you. All the guys do, same as we love them. But it's something totally different than what he and I have as a pair. Hell, Morgan even wrangled him into seeing the dentist somehow! He still won't tell me how you did that."

Morgan didn't reveal their secret, though she and Kayla nodded their agreement.

"I admit, not being there when the guys took you screwed with my head a little. I started to wonder if Mike enjoyed himself more with you than me or if he might start to expect a new flavor every week. I don't think that's healthy for our relationship." Kate showed all her cards. "This way, it's not that different from what we talked about the other day, really. You know, swapping when we're together. Except every once in a while we'd take turns letting someone have all the attention. And that's putting it more simply than I mean to. I'm not trying to brush this off. Life is a constant jumble of priorities and unexpected shit. If we stick together, we can even out the peaks and valleys, make life better for all of us, you know?"

Morgan raised her hand sheepishly.

Devon whacked her on the butt with a dishtowel for the ridiculous propriety.

"I agree with you in theory." Morgan winced. "I'll never forget the heat in Joe's stare when he watched Dave, Neil and James playing with me. Hell, I retired that cake recipe. It could never taste as good as when I shared it with the crew. And Joe told me Mike was actually the one to suck him off at the end the other day. Damn do I regret not seeing that for myself, by the way. But for the first time, I got a little case of jitters. I think you're right. It's best if we reserve five-on-one for times we're all present. And...playing devil's advocate here...we haven't actually tried swapping yet. What if we do and someone finds out they can't handle it?"

"Then we'll discuss and reconsider." Kate made sure to make eye contact with each of her friends. "I couldn't bear to break what we have now. It's a good thing. I think everyone has to know this is a risk-free environment. Everyone's in or no one is. Agreed?"

Each of the women nodded in turn.

When they got to Kayla, she nodded too. Still, Devon could tell the naturist had something else on her mind. "Spit it out, Kay."

"What if it's not five-on-one? What if it's eight-on-one?" The usually brash woman spoke so softly, Devon wasn't sure everyone had heard. "And I'm not just talking about the *guys'* birthdays either."

"To be frank, I'm not sure I'm ready for that, Kay." Morgan interjected before Devon could process the idea of such hedonistic gluttony. "I might never be. Like Neil and his no-BJ rule. But I would like to observe. And I don't begrudge you the request if it's something you're interested in and the other girls are too. Who knows, maybe after I see it for myself, I'll change my mind. I hope you don't count on that, though. Is that okay?"

Kayla hugged Morgan. "I would never pressure you into something you didn't enjoy. But thanks for understanding."

"This is exactly what I hoped for." Kate broke the lingering weight of the moment with a huge grin and a clap. Then she ticked off their agreements on her fingers. "When intact couples are together, like me and Mike over at Morgan and Joe's house or all nine of us here today, anything goes. Birthday girls and boys name their pleasure. Anyone who agrees is in. Anyone who doesn't feel like playing can stay and watch or leave, no hard feelings. None of us will ever judge. We swear to be open and honest if something makes us uncomfortable. What do you think?"

Each of them took time to really consider. This wasn't a fling or some crazy college experiment. These were their lives—their hearts, their soulmates, their futures—they were talking about.

"I think it sucks ass that my birthday was last month and I gotta wait a whole year for my turn." Kayla plumped out her lower lip.

"Ohh, good call." Kate grinned. "Mine is coming up soon. Neener neener."

"Lucky thing our birthdays happen to be distributed pretty evenly throughout the year. Otherwise we might develop some chaffage." Devon giggled.

The women linked hands with their neighbors until they made one continuous, unbroken ring. And with that, the promise was sealed.

"Time to celebrate." Kayla grinned.

"Does anyone have condoms?" Morgan confessed, "I'm wearing a diaphragm, like Kate said she's been doing when we play together, but I haven't been taking my birth control for a while. Mike and Kate aren't the only ones hoping for a miracle."

The friends squealed and fussed over each other. In the meantime, Kayla retrieved a jumbo box of rubbers in various colors and flavors from the bathroom and plunked it on the counter.

Devon raised her eyebrows at the mega-assortment.

"What?" Kay whistled innocently. "They're smart to have on hand for guests in the resort. Okay, plus I figured it wise to be prepared since we seem to gravitate toward my house for our sessions. I swear. Being a naturist is *not* about getting it on at every opportunity. That's your faults."

She wagged her finger at each of them, cracking up the whole time.

"Can I ask a favor?" Kate beamed when the women all nodded without reservation. "Mike is pretty far behind in the sharing space. The closest he came was granting Dev her wish the other day. Would you mind if we made his day?"

"You want to team up on him?" Morgan grinned.

"I'd love to see him speechless for once." Devon chaffed her hands together. "Let's do it."

"I'm in, too." Kayla winked at Kate. "Settle down, I think I see him coming in right now."

They giggled as they peeked through the kitchen window. Sure enough, he headed straight for their trap.

"Why do you ladies look like you're up to no good?" Mike crossed to the sink and filled a bottle with chilled well water. The filtration unit he'd helped Dave install ensured the taste was great direct from the tap.

All four of the women gawked as he slammed the refreshment. His throat flexed in time to his gulps. He sighed and placed the re-emptied container on the counter. When he turned and caught them staring, he swiped the back of his hand over his lips. "What? Did I drool on myself or something?"

He dusted at the front of his fitted T-shirt. Not a single droplet had escaped his mouth.

Pacing, he took a few steps one way, then a couple back. Their gazes tracked his every move.

"Oh. It's like that, is it?" The corners of his mouth kicked up in a self-assured smile that had Devon squirming in her seat. He locked his stare on his wife, who nodded. "Today's the day, huh? Where are the rest of your guys when I need them? Some crew. Abandoning me to the clutches of four horny women. Then again, maybe that's not a terrible fate."

He stalked toward their assembly, his eyes flicking from woman to woman to woman to woman. No one uttered a peep.

"Am I dreaming or do I really have you all to myself for a bit?" He stripped his shirt over his head and dropped it on the slate floor tiles.

Morgan began to clarify.

Mike waved her off. "The rest of them are about five minutes behind. They were wrapping up a few things and shooed me from helping. Let's teach them a lesson about keeping you waiting."

Devon couldn't deny his rugged grace and beauty. Neither could Morgan, apparently. She reached out and tentatively traced the ridge that stretched from his hipbone to disappear beneath the waistband of his low-riding jeans.

He trapped her fingers against his taut belly, then slid their joined hands into his pants. All the while, he never once glanced away from his wife. Kate used his belt to tug him closer. She kissed him as Morgan circled around to hover by his right side.

Mike groaned into Kate's mouth while Morgan unbuckled his belt. With the leather free, nothing held the fabric over his slim hips. Jeans crumpled at their feet. Devon couldn't stay still a moment longer. She abandoned her perch at the bar and stepped behind Mike.

She plastered herself against his back, her hands reaching around to roam over his defined chest while she hugged him from behind. If nothing else, she hoped he realized how much she appreciated the family he'd built and invited her to join. Because of this man, their construction foreman and the head of their gang, they'd each found a place where their individual and collective needs were met.

A row of kisses down his spine made him shiver in her hold. Or maybe his reaction was caused by Morgan and Kayla descending in front of him, stroking, licking and nibbling as they sank to their knees in unison. Having such a strong man in their clutches, causing his legs to wobble with their attention, sent a rush of adrenaline through Devon's veins.

She smacked his ass playfully yet hard enough to sting. She liked the evidence left behind in the form of her glowing handprint. It looked so small on his firm butt.

"Behave yourself, shorty." He grinned over his shoulder.

Whatever else he might have threatened dissolved into a gurgle. Devon craned her neck around his ribs to see what had caused such a guttural cry. Kate's lips were nestled against the base of his cock while Kayla massaged his balls.

When his wife pulled off his shaft, pressing a kiss to the tip, she wrapped her fist around it and aimed it toward Morgan. "Go ahead."

Kate's best friend whimpered. She looked at Kate, then Mike, then his cock.

They all held their breath.

"Now or never," she whispered before opening her mouth and leaning forward. Kate guided Mike's cock between her lips.

Tense, she choked a little. Devon laid a hand on her shoulder and kneaded the knot there. As Morgan relaxed, she took more of the foreman into her mouth. Soon her lips rested on Kate's knuckles.

Mike cursed. "Jesus, that's sweet. You're amazing. All of you. Hope you don't expect me to last like this."

Devon giggled as she angled herself more toward his side. He wrapped an arm around her shoulders. She suspected the gesture had more to do with keeping his balance than embracing her, though she didn't begrudge him the assistance.

Kate and Morgan took turns laving, sucking and stroking Mike's cock while Kayla perfected the motion of her relentless fingers over his sac. Devon felt like she should help, but even when Mike widened his stance, she didn't have any room to maneuver.

The next time Morgan descended on Mike, Kate glanced up. "Dev, let Kay suck on your fingers for a minute."

Turned on beyond belief, she wasn't about to argue. She extended her hand without question. Her friend smiled before taking the digits into her mouth. Devon couldn't help but squirm when Kay's wet tongue snaked around her knuckles, slathering them with saliva and making zillions of nerve endings stand at attention.

"Oh yeah, not so tough now, are you?" Mike squeezed her tight to his torso. "That's fucking hot. Shit."

She retaliated by scraping her teeth over his nipple. The tight disc couldn't have been in a better position for her to reach. He released a long, low moan. His head tipped back, and she saw his lips moving out of the corner of her eye as if he prayed for stamina or maybe thanked the stars for shining such good fortune on them.

Kate let him suffer while she relieved Morgan. In between their active duty, the women licked and nipped his abdomen or studied their friend as they imparted pleasure. Kayla never faltered in her dual manipulation of Mike's balls and Devon's fingers. She was an expert after all.

Next time Morgan nudged Kate from their shared treat, the foreman's wife developed an evil grin. "Enough, Kay. I think they're ready."

Devon glanced between Kayla, Kate and Mike. Could she mean…?

"Yeah." Kate nodded. "I'll let you in on a little secret. Mike might prefer to be the one doing the fucking, but when I use my fingers on him while blowing him… Let's just say the results are pretty spectacular."

"Fuck me." Mike swayed. Together they managed to brace him.

"Yeah, that's kind of the point." Kayla rubbed the side of his ass closest to her. She filled her palm with the solid muscle and gently pulled it toward her.

"You can find his prostate?" Kate smirked up at Devon.

"You have met my guys, right?" She rolled her eyes. "I might have done this once or twice before."

"I knew you were the right woman for the job." Kate entrusted her husband's satisfaction to Devon. She resumed licking him as if he were the best-tasting lollipop in the world.

"Be gentle with me," Mike half-teased. The corners of his mouth pinched at the first glancing contact of her fingertip sliding along his crack.

"Promise." She suckled his chest lightly while she traced his puckered hole with slow circles, painting Kayla's spit over the entrance.

"Her hands are miniature." Morgan petted his corded thigh. "You probably won't even realize she's inside you."

His huff when Devon pressed inward, breaching the tight ring of muscle guarding his ass, proclaimed otherwise.

"Or not." Morgan chuckled before engulfing him once more.

"That's right, Mike. Let Devon in. She's going to make you feel so good," Kate murmured to her husband.

"Already is." He grunted. "All of you are. Always do."

"We love you too." Kayla nuzzled his hip.

Devon took advantage of his distraction to penetrate completely. As she moved, he began to relax, loosen, allowing her to angle her hand. She stroked in and out, curling her fingers into the come-hither shape that usually did the trick for James and Neil.

She knew she had it right when he cursed a blue streak and twitched his hips first forward, then back hard. His cock slipped from Morgan's lips with a wet smack. Kate was quick to welcome him into her mouth again, sucking with enough pressure to hollow her cheeks.

Devon rubbed Mike's chest and belly to calm him as she continued to prod the chestnut-sized organ in time to his wife's quickening migrations up and down his solid shaft.

"Are you going to be a good boy and come for us?" Morgan impressed Devon with her schoolmarm act. "You know we like it when you show us how much we turn you on."

"Holy. Shit. Holy shit." Dave stutter-stepped as he entered the room, naked as always once inside. "Sign me up for the next turn. I know what I want for my birthday, and Christmas. Every year. Until I die."

"What the fu—" Joe crashed into him from behind. He peeked over Dave's shoulder, then growled, "Son of a bitch. Me too."

James skirted around them for a better view of the action. "I could get into that. I think it should be a new crew tradition. Whoever's celebrating can be the center of attention."

"I wanna party. A lot." Neil didn't stop with the rest of his friends. He barreled toward the action like a young boy cannonballing into a lake on the first day of summer vacation.

"Funny you should say that." Kayla grinned up at them from her place at Mike's feet. "We sort of decided something similar."

"Can we...talk...about...it later?" Mike's chest heaved between each forced phrase.

Dave approached from behind. He looped his arms around Mike's middle, supporting his friend without interrupting Devon's devilish handiwork.

"That good, huh?" Dave grinned. "It's not every day you come apart like this, foreman. You've got quite an audience now. Why don't you show us what a fucking lucky bastard you are?"

Devon could feel energy sparking through the room, arcing in glowing connections between each of the nine of them in every possible permutation. She knew right then they'd made the right choice. Having all of them together made this so much...more.

Mike didn't stand a chance.

She tapped his prostate in a syncopated rhythm Neil had taught her to drive James wild. It worked just as well on their boss.

Neil and James chanted encouragement to her as the other guys did the same for their wives. In less than a minute, Mike shouted. His fists balled as though he struggled to keep from exploding. He thrust his hips into the air, his ass clenching around her fingers. Then he shook in Dave's hold like he'd grabbed the exposed end of a live 220 wire.

"Fuck, yes." Neil encouraged him. "Shoot all over them. Make them yours. Ours."

Only then did Devon realize Kate, Morgan and Kayla had huddled together, their faces side by side. Mike's cock had tugged from their lips with his involuntary shudders.

Slipping her hand from his body, she joined her friends in a semi-circle. Dave helped ensure each of them received at least one spurt of his come, adorning them with the results of their hard work.

When the foremen went limp, Dave allowed him to succumb to gravity, easing their weight onto the floor. He cradled his friend through the final throes of his rapture.

The rest of the crew descended on their women. Joe nearly tackled Morgan, who'd taken the brunt of Mike's orgasm. He snuffed the flicker of doubt Devon caught in her eyes when he kissed her madly, pausing only to lick her chin and neck clean.

James and Neil swarmed Devon. They had her feeling a little like a bone between two dogs when they both attempted to devour the droplets of Mike's semen on her cheeks.

The delicacy didn't last long. The guys had moved on, demonstrating exactly how much they'd enjoyed the scene they'd walked in on, when Kate's voice rose above the din caused by a cacophony of moans, sighs and pleas.

"Hang on a minute." She shushed their objections. "While you boys were outside playing, we decided it's time to take things up a notch."

The crew shot each other a round of worried looks.

"What could be more intense than that?" Neil nudged Mike with his foot. The foreman groaned, then shifted, his heavy eyelids rising slowly. "I think you might have killed him."

"Ladies, move over one couple to your right."

Devon kissed each of her guys on the cheek, laughing at the stunned expressions on their faces. "Have fun. See you in a bit."

She extricated herself from their limbs, regretting the loss of their heat, their touch, their love for a second. Until she sank into Joe's open arms, straddling his thighs. "Hi."

"Hi." He looked to Morgan for permission.

"It's all right." She smiled. "Probably only fair since I just gave your best friend a killer blowjob."

"Ohmigod." He clapped his hand over his mouth, but not before the rest of the guys ragged on him.

"What are you, a thirteen-year-old girl?" James cracked up.

"Hey, cut him some slack." Mike perked up as Kayla snuggled beside him on the carpet. "I can promise these ladies will make you forget your own name. Never mind that you're a grown man who should have some fucking pride."

"You held out longer than I thought you would, if that's any consolation," Morgan teased from her place in Dave's clutches.

Neil lifted Kate into his arms. "I hope you don't mind if I take you someplace a little more comfortable?"

"Suit up first." She jerked her chin toward the condom stash. "Anyone who's with Morgan has to wear one too."

"Are we supposed to use all of those?" His eyes got round.

"Maybe eventually." She laughed. "But hopefully we'll be pregnant long before then and we won't need to bother anymore."

"Good plan." Neil tossed two packets to each of the guys. He sheathed first James, then himself in record time. When he finished, he glanced over at Mike, who began to rouse from the daze they'd knocked him into. "Get on that, buddy, would you?"

"Sure, sure." He waved them off.

Kate giggled when Neil scooped her up once more. She trailed her fingers down his neck. "Coming, James?"

"I have a tiny bit more control than that, Katiebug."

Devon smiled as her guys toyed with her friend. James had told her once about how Kate had really cemented the crew together in the beginning. She would never forget that Kate had eased James's lingering worries about his sexuality and granted him acceptance to grow into the man he was today. Though they'd always been best friends, the guys had benefited from the women they'd pulled into their group, who had provided the extra emotional something they hadn't realized they were missing.

If it hadn't been for Kate, Devon suspected their group might have fractured or drifted apart. They'd grown so much. Shared so much. It was impossible to separate them anymore.

"Shh..." Joe's hush made her wonder if she'd actually whimpered for her pair. "We'll go with your guys. You can play voyeur if you want."

As if settling on a plan, the crewmembers each embraced their new partner and claimed a spot in the adjoining space. Neil and James had laid out Kate on the couch. James supported her shoulders while Neil pressed her knees apart with his shoulders. He burrowed between her thighs, intent on tasting her.

Dave sat in the loveseat with Morgan straddling his lap. She left room for him to roll purple latex over his thick erection. When he finished, she snuggled close to his broad chest. He kissed her cheek and spoke in a soothing murmur. Too low for Devon to make out exactly what he was saying, the general rumble of his bass sounded nice to her.

Joe opted to bend her over the coffee table in the center of the room. His warm chest blanketed her back, and his cock rode the furrow of her pussy when he reached beneath her to cup her breasts and prevent her belly from pressing to the cool surface of the furnishing. She couldn't say she minded when she had a panoramic view of the action around her.

Even Mike recovered enough to carry Kay and deposit her onto the rug in front of the fireplace. He stretched out behind her, caressing her from her shoulder along her ribs to the curve of her hip. He extended his arm for her to rest her head on, then snaked his other hand around her torso, sheltering her and keeping her close to his body.

They turned their faces toward each other to exchange a frisky kiss complete with Kayla nibbling on his bottom lip. "You know, you would look hot if you got this pierced. A little stud, right in the center."

"I think I'll leave that stuff to you and Dave." He laughed. "Though I have to say, I've always loved the way your hardware looks. It fits you perfectly."

As if to prove his point, he thumbed the silver in her breasts.

"They're not just for show, you know." She sighed. "That feels twice as good as it used to. Tug on the hoops. Please."

Mike groaned. "Damn. I thought I'd never be hard again. It took you less than five minutes to prove me wrong."

He scanned the entire room as he proclaimed their victory.

Devon met his wandering gaze and smirked. Her smugness evaporated when Joe bounced his cock against her clit. She clutched the edges of the coffee table as though she might fly around the room like a rogue helium balloon if she didn't anchor herself.

"I always thought it would be fun to tease you, Dev." He dragged his fingertips from her shoulders to her ass in maddening, erratic patterns. "You're such an imp. And the pranks you pull... You're a disobedient pixie. It turns me on when your guys focus all that extra energy. I always wanted to try it and see if I could too."

"You're doing a pretty good job." Neil lifted his mouth from where he toyed with Kate's pussy. "Looks like you have her full attention now."

"Do I?" Joe covered her, nibbling at her ear.

"Yes," she mewled.

"Good." He gripped her hip easily with one hand, then reached between them with the other. "Because I want you to know who it is taking you, Dev. When we work together or when we hang out, you'll know that I've had you and you've had me. You can count on me. Come to me with anything. I'll always have your back like I do now. And if Morgan or I need to borrow some of your light and fun, you always know. You share your brightness with all of us around you. I love that about you."

Devon didn't expect the wash of emotion he inspired in her. Not like this. Not so strong. She couldn't speak around the lump in her throat. So instead she reached down, between her legs, and lifted him to the threshold of her body. She held him there.

"Thank you," he whispered before he advanced.

The introduction of his flesh into hers shocked a gasp from her. Heat and pressure built until his head slipped inside. When she thought she might cry uncle and tell him he was too much, a familiar hand landed on her upper arm.

James.

"Give it a second." He promised, "You're going to love it. He's so smooth when he fucks. Just like he talks."

Morgan cried out from where she nestled tighter onto Dave's lap. Whether because their friend's large cock stretched her or because the discussion of her husband fueled the flames, Devon couldn't be sure.

"Damn, Mike wasn't exaggerating. You're so fucking tight." Joe huffed as he slowed his invasion. "You'd better go slow when you get to Dave. Maybe save him for another day."

Devon knew she wouldn't. After bonding with Joe and Mike, she couldn't leave the other man out in the cold.

Conversations flared, interspersed with moans, sighs and the slick slaps of good sex. The other women exchanged connections with their temporary partners the same as she had with Joe. They had so many of these compatible features—intertwined lives, hopes, interests and fantasies—that each combination resulted in something new and wonderful. Her heart glowed with serenity. She'd never felt as safe as she did surrounded by her eight best friends.

She looked up to see James kneeling above Kate, who pampered him with what looked like one hell of a hummer. He played with his nipples and muttered encouragement while he stared at Neil. Their mate had climbed Kate's body and pressed inside. Devon's pussy clenched when the guys exchanged a sultry kiss, connecting all three of them in a lusty triangle.

Kayla cried out, drawing Devon's stare. The landscape was like a licentious feast, every course holding another delicious treat for her to devour. Mike held Kay's jaw at the perfect angle to grant himself access to her mouth. He kissed her hard and a little rough as he slid his other hand between her legs to play with her clit. She responded by opening herself to him, raising her leg to allow him to lunge deeper, faster, between her thighs.

Joe smacked Devon's ass and increased his pace. "Dirty girl. You like spying on them, don't you?"

"Yes." She squealed when he repeated the spank on the other side. The tingles left by his palm enhanced her arousal, making it effervesce like champagne.

"Keep watching." He stayed true to James's promise, gliding in her from root to tip, careful not to hurt her yet refusing to skimp on his thrusts. "I can feel your pussy fluttering around me. Getting stronger now. Especially when I rub my cock here."

He repeated the motion until they both were gasping for air.

Morgan shouted, "I'm going to come."

Joe froze for a second.

"Yeah, look." Devon figured he'd earned a little teasing of his own. "See how wild she is for your friend? Her hair looks gorgeous waving down her back while she rides him."

Joe landed another smack on her ass. And that was all it took.

Devon heard the escalating cries of the other women even as she surrendered to her climax. She stared into James's eyes as another man showered her with bliss. Except it didn't feel like that. Not really. Joe was part of the crew, same as Neil and James. An extension of her lovers, he treated her as his own.

Before she'd quite wrung all the possible rapture from his cock, Joe withdrew. "Sorry, sweetheart. I couldn't stay or I'd lose it. And somehow I don't think that's the plan."

She hadn't recovered enough to argue. Instead, when he traced her lips with his index finger, she sucked on the tip like a baby with a pacifier. The pulls of her mouth matched the aftershocks wringing her pussy.

Before she could cool down, Mike took the reins.

"Trade women," he ordered.

Joe kissed her cheek, then smiled. "See you later."

Before she could figure out where she was supposed to be, Mike snatched her around the waist and yanked her to him. Lying on her side, she observed Kate slumped in Dave's lap. He changed his condom discretely while she recovered from the wreckage Devon knew James and Neil were capable of inflicting on a woman's reserve.

Morgan squealed when Neil got cozy between her legs and started the process of reawakening her arousal. As if they'd hit rewind, the guys seduced their new partners in the same manner they had the first. Devon could relate when Kayla yelped at the first tap of Joe's cock on her clit.

Unlike the day on the job site, Mike slid into her with relative ease. "Ah, that's better. I guess I should have had Joe work you open for me last time too."

Devon was used to being fucked twice in a row. There were plenty of nights both James and Neil took a turn or two or three, one of them recovering while the other continued to raise her higher and higher. She concentrated on the spark of pleasure in her core and allowed Mike to fan it back to life. Apparently, the other women had similar experience.

Before long, a chorus of *fuck yeah* and *harder* and *right there* accompanied their moans. This round went faster, as the women had been primed by their previous lovers. They took pity on the men, who each managed to cling to their control long enough to grant his partner release.

Devon still floated when Mike called, "One more time. We can do it. Hurry."

Dave came to claim her. He flopped into the loveseat, draping her over him. "It's okay if you're not comfortable, Dev. Let me keep you close. That'll be enough. Rub your clit on my cock and I bet we'll both come in no time. Hell, I'll be lucky to last through a minute of outercourse at this point."

"I didn't know you were into frottage." She sighed at the mental movies that thought inspired, adding the demand to her birthday wish list. A fetish for another time.

The gentle giant held her as though she were made of spun glass. That wouldn't do at all.

"Stop talking, Dave." She put her hand over his mouth. He always rambled when nerves plagued him, which happened more often than she would have guessed in the early days of their friendship. Kayla calmed him with her easy acceptance, massage skills and naturist philosophy. It was a good match. No, a perfect one.

Somehow, Devon realized lately that of all the men, she could boss Dave around a bit. Not that she would manipulate him, or take advantage, but sometimes, it helped break him out of a mental rut. He bit his bottom lip and scrunched his eyes closed. His cock throbbed against her belly. She had no doubt he'd let guilt and fear keep him from the ultimate relief he so desperately needed if she didn't interject.

"Put your hands on the arms of the chair." She had never used such a stern tone before. With this man, in this time and place, it felt right. So she did it again. "Don't move them unless I tell you to."

"Dev?" He did as she asked despite the questions in his eyes.

"The biggest tamed by the smallest." Joe chuckled as he filled Kate. "Never thought I'd see the day. Son of a bitch, that's sexy."

"And so are you." Kate smiled up at Joe. They had such an easy friendship. Both of them people people. Both nurturers by nature. They loved to see their family happy and fed off the positive karma in the room. "I can't wait to hear you erupting inside me. I bet you flood that condom."

151

"Fuck." Neil skipped laving Kayla's engorged pussy and went straight to riding her. "I owe you a raincheck, hon. I can't wait."

"It's been too long since the last time we did this." She wrapped her legs around him, welcoming him inside.

"Won't make that mistake again." He tipped her face toward James's cock. Ruddy and painfully erect, it jutted into the air. "Now show James how much you missed him."

Kayla fulfilled his wish by entwining her fingers with James's. The two of them shared a bond so emotional it was almost spiritual. Devon had never seen two people be able to sit in comfortable silence as long as these two, whether it was on the deck, watching the lake or while listening to the rowdy crew at a dinner party.

"Same goes, Kay." James squeezed her hand. "But I'm dying here. Please?"

She opened her mouth and welcomed him inside before he'd finished asking.

Devon had to hurry or she wouldn't have time to recover and come with the others. It would hurt at least a little. She didn't mind. Rising onto her knees, she grabbed hold of Dave's cock and positioned it so she could slide onto the extra-thick shaft.

Fortunately, her two previous orgasms had generated a ton of lube.

Still he lodged in her, barely an inch deep.

"Dev, don't." Dave started to shift.

"Did I tell you to move?" She arrowed a disapproving frown in his direction.

"Sorry, sorry." His cock twitched between her stretched pussy lips. "And quit doing that if you want to have any hope at all of me finishing this race."

"Oh no, you're not allowed to surrender until I tell you." She had no idea this side of her even existed. But with him, it did. And now that she'd found it, she decided she liked it.

He nodded once.

"That's brilliant." Mike's awed murmur reached her ears as she hitched her hips to lift up a bit. Once she'd slicked Dave's shaft, she sank down, letting inertia force her onto him farther. It burned. She wouldn't deny that. But she kind of liked it.

Devon braced her hands behind her on Dave's knees. She whimpered, then granted him permission to touch her. "Rub my clit."

He did, in such a perfect pattern she feared she'd come too soon.

"Not so fast."

He slowed instantly.

The rush of exhilaration his obedience brought helped her to work him deeper.

"You've almost got him, babe." Neil called reassurance as he rocked into Kayla. "Kay loves seeing it too. She's smothering my cock. Damn. So amazing. Both of you."

Their support gave her the strength to continue.

"I'm not going to break." She smiled into Dave's uncertain eyes. "Hold me. Kiss me."

He did. His broad hands covered most of her back as he tugged her to him. The more severe angle allowed her weight to press her the rest of the way onto his cock. White, searing pleasure mixed with pain flashed before her.

When it could easily have stolen her buzz, he neutralized the intensity with the cool, refreshing gentleness of his lips. Next to James, he was easily the best kisser of the crew. He made love to her mouth. Reverent and patient, he morphed her discomfort into ecstasy.

Once united, they hardly had to move to incite a riot of sensation in each other.

Dave went up for air.

She used the tiny separation to pat his chest. "Such a good boy."

"Not if you keep talking." His head dropped back against the cushion of the loveseat. "I'll break your don't-shoot edict pretty fucking fast."

If the desperate shouts behind her were any indication, Devon figured the whole crew rowed in the same boat.

"Oh, really?" She tapped his cheek with her open palm. "Maybe you want me to punish you next time around."

"Serious, Dev." The cords in his neck stood out and the corner of his eye twitched. "On the edge."

And suddenly so was she. He filled her beyond belief yet handed over every ounce of authority without flinching. No one deferred to her that easily. Youthful and tiny, she was too easy to dismiss. Maybe that was what she loved about Dave. He'd never done that to her. His size probably made him all too aware of how much people assumed based on appearance.

How many people had expected him to be bold and in control simply because he was huge? She'd give him this if she could.

"I'll tie you up and ask Joe to teach me how to spank you properly." She bit his lip.

"No, no, no." He might have denied it, but his cock bulged. It said, *yes, yes, yes.*

"You're going to break. Do it." She set him free. "Come inside me. There's no room left. You're going to make us sloppy. Flood me. Force it out around us so it soaks your balls."

Devon had no idea where the stream of graphic portends came from. Dave seemed to appreciate it, though. He roared. His eyes flew open wider and his head snapped up. Across the room, Kayla screamed. James and Neil too. The cycle of shared desire paid forward to her as Dave capitulated.

He fucked upward with short jabs as he overflowed her pussy with gushes of semen. His hands locked on to her shoulders, pulling her tight. The juncture of their bodies ensured her clit strummed across his hard muscles.

An orgasm of epic proportions threatened to rip her apart.

Through the typhoon of emotion and sensation, she heard Mike, Morgan, Kate and Joe join them in release. Together they celebrated their bonds. To each other—their spouses, their friends and their lovers.

When Devon floated back to Earth, a long time later, she realized they'd ended up on the rug in front of the fire. Their heads all together, they lay in a circle with their bodies pointed out like the spokes on a wheel or maybe the rays of a glorious star.

James held her and Neil held him. Behind her guys was another couple and another and another. Or maybe that last one was in front of her. They snuggled in an infinite loop.

Someone whispered, "I love you."

They all echoed the sentiment.

CHAPTER SEVEN

The twenty-seventh of January came pretty damn quick. Dave hadn't looked forward to his birthday this much since he'd turned seven. That year, his father had promised him a red Schwinn if he was good— also known as staying quiet and fetching more beers whenever the jerk's current drink came close to empty. He always figured he must not have made the grade. Either that or the old man had been too hammered to remember his bribe by the time Dave's birthday rolled around.

But today had the potential to make up for all of that disappointment and then some.

The crew had shared his favorite dinner, then put candles on one of Morgan's sinful creations and even sang him a horribly off-key rendition of the birthday song. Still, he drummed his fingers on the table, barely containing his anticipation.

"I think somebody better suck this guy off before he explodes," Mike joked when he caught the raging hard-on pointing straight up on Dave's belly beneath the bar. "So what's it going to be, Davey-boy? An eight-person BJ?"

Since they'd held the party at his and Kay's house, everyone was already naked. Saved time too. He liked being efficient.

"What if I don't want to be the centerpiece?" He scrubbed his cheeks, unable to believe something so ridiculous would pop out of his mouth.

"Then I'd say there's a hospital twenty minutes down the mountain. We should take you to the emergency room and find out what's wrong." Joe's raised eyebrows would be comical if so much didn't ride on the line.

"It's *my* birthday. I think I should decide what I want my present to be." Dave tapped one finger on his cheek.

"Uh, you're turning down a chance to be ravaged like a dirty piñata at this soirée?" Neil looked at him like he'd gone crazy. "We're talking about four gorgeous, horny women and guys willing to suck, fuck or bend over for your beast of a cock."

Dave *thunked* his forehead onto his curled fist. "You're not helping."

"What *do* you want?" Mike stared at Dave, then smirked. "I can only think of one thing better than being the centerpiece."

"Yeah." He nodded. "That."

***

Crewmates exchanged glances. Devon still didn't understand their silent communication. "Okay, stop with that spidey-sense shit. What's going on here?"

"I'd rather give my present to Kay." Dave slipped from the barstool to crouch next to Devon's chair. "I'd love to watch you and her together."

Caught off guard, Devon sputtered. Neil and James flanked her in an instant. Their erections seemed to second Dave's proposal.

"Are you positive?" Kayla tugged Dave to face her. "You've never seen me with another woman."

"Exactly. I'd sure as hell like to remedy that."

"No, seriously." Kay wouldn't let him misdirect her concern.

"I know what it's like when I need one of the guys. It's a fire that starts low and dim but builds until it's raging out of control. As much as I love you and want you with a ferocity that will never die, you can't give me that. Do you know what it's like to know there's something you need that I can't give you? Something you're not getting at all? It's been growing

161

stronger lately. You wake me when you dream about it. You cry out in your sleep. I could tell how bad you wanted it the day we swapped partners. I'll help you however I can. You don't have to hide your needs from me."

Kayla didn't deny his claims.

He returned his focus to Devon, clasping her tiny hand between his. "*You* can do this for her. For both of you. I see it in your eyes when you're near her. You wonder...like I used to before I met Mike. Please. That's all I want for my birthday. Make my wife happy. Yourself too. Please."

"Dave..." Kayla might have said more if tears hadn't sheened her eyes and clogged her throat.

"It's okay, baby." He tugged her into his lap and nuzzled her neck. "I understand. Totally. I do. Let me give you this. And if Devon can't, we'll find someone else."

"I love you." Kayla smothered him with kisses.

Devon wondered if the couple would forget about the rest of the crew, who admired their friends and shared in the harmony they generated. She stamped out the wave of jealousy that Dave's promise to Kay had instilled. She didn't care to think of someone outside their circle with her friend. Silly, yet true.

"I love you too." Dave finally broke their make out session, his forehead resting on Kay's as they both attempted to catch their breath. "Now get over there and seduce that girl before she balks again. You're so sexy you'll have her tripping over her own tongue if you quit holding back. I should know."

Kayla grinned. She hugged Dave tight, then climbed off his lap.

Air whooshed from Devon's lungs when the alluring naturist focused her attention on Dev like a laser beam.

"Holy shit," Mike cursed under his breath as Kay stalked closer. From the corner of her eye, Devon saw Kate and Morgan shove their men to the couch and kneel between their knees. If they were going to put on a show, she'd better make it good.

"Will you go easy on me because I'm a virgin?" Devon did her best imitation of a simper.

"Not likely." Kayla's feral grin shot adrenaline straight into Devon's heart. It beat a crazy tattoo against her ribs. "It's been too long."

Devon nodded. "I should have approached you after Kate's wedding, but we were tipsy and I didn't want it to go down like that. With readymade excuses, I mean. And then I got scared. I couldn't stand the idea of ruining our friendship. The more time that passed, the weirder it seemed to bring it up."

"You think too much." Kayla closed the last of the space between them. She wrapped Devon in a tender hug. Softness to softness. That alone rocked her world, so different than the firm men who'd come up behind her.

Trapped between the heat and hardness of her men and the gentle warmth Kayla generated, Devon had no chance at escape, not that she wished for one. Dave couldn't resist approaching for a close-up view of the action. He cuddled up to his wife's back, supporting her as she embarked on a new adventure. The three men slung their arms over each other's shoulders, forming a larger ring around the two women who embraced at their center.

Utterly protected, Devon felt free to explore.

"Kiss me," Kayla whispered. "So I know you need this too. It's not my desire coloring the situation, is it?"

"You've worried you're imagining the chemistry between us?" Devon cursed. "I'm sorry. I didn't realize I put you through that kind of doubt. It's not one-sided, Kay. I've thought about doing this for a long time."

Devon stood on her tiptoes. She looped her hands around Kayla's neck and tugged until the statuesque woman bent. Their mouths lingered a hairsbreadth apart for the span of several heartbeats. Dev could smell Kay's signature organic cherry lip balm from this close. She reached out her tongue and stole a tiny taste.

Kayla's lips parted on a sigh.

That sweet, simple sound of relief was all it took to motivate Devon. She rocked forward, sealing her mouth over Kay's. The other woman responded immediately. Not with the vicious insistence of one of the crewmen when they were taunted beyond their control. Rather with an aching tenderness that inflamed Devon all the more for its affectionate restraint.

Kayla nestled their lips together with gentle caresses that had goose bumps dotting Devon's skin and raising the blond hairs on her arms. Kissing a woman was nothing like kissing a guy. She couldn't tell if it was Neil, Dave, James or some combination of all three that chaffed her with consistent brushes of their hands that only revved her higher.

Pleasure suffused her being as she sank deeper into the fine, delicate kiss. It reminded her of the first time she'd framed a house and knew she'd become hopelessly addicted to the experience. Awe ran rampant through her system.

Kayla flirted with Devon's mouth, employing tiny licks and nips. When she sucked lightly on Devon's lower lip, she thought she might orgasm from kissing alone. So much attention was paid to each glance of tongue and teeth, the simple exchange mutated into a complex symphony of passion.

"Damn." The reverent curse sounded like it came from Joe. Devon peeked in his direction long enough to discern the slow bobbing of Morgan's head in his lap. Beside him, Mike enjoyed similar treatment as they watched the show. "That's *so* fucking sweet."

Devon agreed one-hundred percent. She found herself needing more. When she writhed against Kayla's lush frame, her friend grinned where their mouths were still joined.

"You're easy, Dev," she whispered. "I figured it'd take me at least five or ten minutes to have you begging."

"Bitch." Devon tweaked the nipple ring gracing her friend's breast. She'd often admired the jewelry, and wondered if it enhanced her pleasure as much as it seemed to when her husband flicked his tongue around the fittings and tugged them gently with his teeth.

If Kay's sharp inhalation was any indication, the answer was a resounding yes. She'd have to remember to ask Kay later who'd done them for her and if she'd accompany Devon for an appointment. She'd grown so much over the past year since she'd met the crew she could hardly believe how much of herself she'd hidden away. For the first time, she felt like she had come into her own.

The *real* Devon.

The complete woman was here to stay.

"Hey." Kayla stroked her cheek with the bent knuckle of her index finger. She separated their mouths long enough to ask, "Still with me? Too much?"

"No." Devon hated the tear that spilled over her friend's hand. "Perfect. Exactly right. I can't believe I wasted so much time."

"Maybe you weren't ready." James petted her back. "When you came to us, we pushed you hard. Fast. It was a lot to adjust to and you did great. You're sure now. Totally confident and so damn flawless I can't begin to deserve you. There's nothing to get in the way or trip you up. I'm so proud of you, Devon."

"We love you," Neil murmured in her other ear. "We're here for you. We have forever. No worries. Just enjoy the moment. No one could understand this better than James and me. It's not always easy to take what you need."

167

"What they said, runt." Dave propped his chin on Kayla's shoulder. "Everything we've shared has led to this moment. Go ahead. Claim your reward."

Devon smiled through her tears. Bundles of nerves unknotted in her gut. She savored Neil and James kissing her neck and the reassurance in Dave's gaze as he presented his wife for their shared pleasure.

This time when their lips collided, it was with greater urgency. The soft, sweet swipes still rocked her world, different completely from the fierce claim one of the men would make on her mouth. Devon shivered when Kayla advanced, pressing their torsos more tightly together. The mounds of her friend's breasts landed above hers.

Dev lowered her hands to Kayla's waist, her fingers grasping at Kay's tight ass, begging for what she wasn't sure.

Mike groaned from behind them. "Give me a minute, Kate, or I'm going to lose it. Let me grab the feather bed from the closet for them. If I can still walk with this monster hard-on."

Musical laughter accompanied the foreman's grumbling. Kate always told them how much she loved to torment her husband. Driving him wild was one of the highlights of her life.

Kayla reclaimed Devon's focus when the other woman planted her palms on Devon's ass. Dev slung one thigh as high on Kay's hip as she could, then hopped. The guys supported her as she clung to Kayla like a baby koala. Both of them moaned when their torsos aligned better.

"Shorty." Kay nipped her chin, then licked a trail down Devon's neck.

She might have been embarrassed about the slickness she painted across Kayla's belly if the other woman hadn't encouraged her to continue her gyrations with that unflinching grip on Devon's rear.

A cool breeze wafted over them, followed by a dull thump that could only come from a thick feather mattress. She'd know that sound anywhere since they'd each agreed to purchase one for their living rooms after their partner-swapping session. They'd had enough of bruised knees and rug burns in critical areas when an innocent movie night turned into one of their smoking group sessions.

The pad bounced a little, knocking into James's and Neil's ankles. The guys tumbled backward onto the puffy surface with matching grunts. Lacking their support, Kayla tipped forward. They landed in a tangle of limbs. Dave piled on for fun, squishing Neil. He also rubbed his rock hard cock against his friend in the process, if their sighs and lusty oaths were any indication.

Kayla and Devon giggled at their antics. They laughed together even as they writhed, their bodies connected from toes to fingertips. Devon spread her legs wider, welcoming Kayla into the cradle of her thighs. The pressure of Kay's pubic bone riding her mound surprised a whimper from her.

"Have you ever wondered about tribbing, Dev?" Kayla whispered in her ear.

"What?" She blushed. "I don't know what that is."

"Don't worry. I'll show you." Kayla rocked against her again. "It's my favorite. Like this. Or scissoring."

Devon didn't care what she called it as long as Kay continued to inject pure pleasure into her veins. They reveled in their clinch, using every part of their bodies to communicate their longing.

"She feels great, doesn't she?" James brushed stray hair from Devon's forehead and tucked it behind her ear. "I love it when your eyes turn dark like this."

"So amazing." She gasped, and dragged her nails from Kay's ass to her shoulders, begging her silently to move.

"More of that later," Kayla promised with another kiss. Each of her touches showcased an economy of motion that concentrated passion to its purest extract. "First, I want to taste you. All of you."

Devon's pussy quivered at the idea. If Kayla ate her out half as well as she kissed, Dev might die of ecstasy overload before the afternoon was over. Because she admitted James had been knocked from that coveted *best kisser* spot by Kay.

Would she expect Devon to return the favor?

She wasn't sure she was ready to be the aggressor yet. She had no skills. What if Kay had waited forever and Devon couldn't deliver a satisfying experience?

"No pressure, Dev." Kayla petted her belly. "It's your first time. Let me make it good for you. Believe me, I'll enjoy this as much as you."

Kay didn't hesitate. She licked a trail down Devon's neck, torturing her with the measured glide of her lips across Dev's collarbone. As though she had a map of all the most sensitive spots along her route, she detoured to every single one. One of the benefits to being with another woman, Devon supposed.

She recalled watching James suck Mike or how Joe could make Neil come in record time by jerking him off while riding him hard. It was clear the men fed off each other but also that they had a better understanding of how to push each other's buttons.

Kayla had the same intrinsic knowledge of Devon's anatomy. She put it to good use. Her fingertips fluttered over the peaks of Dev's breasts, teasing her nipples into hardened pebbles without pinching them too tight.

Kay's ideal manipulation had Devon's chest swollen and aching for more contact. She bucked her hips against Kayla's softly rounded tummy, moaning when her clit slid across the damp skin there.

"In good time, Dev." Kayla continued her unhurried assault. "There's no rush. Though, if you want to come, go ahead. We'll feed off each other's orgasms. It's not like being with a man. Climaxing isn't the end. It's just a peak on the journey to the summit. I bet I could give you a dozen. And the same for you to me."

"Jesus." Neil groaned from where he lounged above Devon's head on the mattress. James angled his face until he could suck their mate a few times from root to tip.

"They're so careful. Slower than molasses," Joe muttered to himself from the couch. He massaged Morgan's head, which lay in his lap as she observed her friends. None of the men would last if they kept up the stimulation. Somehow they all seemed to abstain by some collective order, wanting to share the women's ecstasy. "I would die if I had to hold myself to that pace."

"Nothing like savoring the moment," Kayla mumbled against Devon's breast. She spiraled kisses from the outside curve, growing ever closer to the center. All the while, they swayed against each other, brushing their clits across matching feminine softness.

"She's great. Placid. Precise." Devon forced herself to breathe through another wave of pleasure. They rolled over her rhythmically, each one more forceful than the last.

"Thank you." Kayla paused, lifting her head to make out with Devon again. Their tongues swirled around each other. Devon drew Kayla inside her mouth, twirling the tongue piercing she'd often admired. Kay shuddered.

Devon wrapped her arms around her friend, enfolding her in the steam they generated together. All the while blood rushed to her pussy, which only enhanced the periodic contact she made with Kayla's torso.

"More." She pressed on Kay's shoulders, desperate for relief.

"In time." The other woman smiled as she resumed her ministrations on Devon's other breast. While she dallied, her fingers walked down the flat expanse of Devon's belly. Need had her abdomen clenched tight. "Relax, Dev."

She tried. Nothing she did worked. Her appetite had grown too long. "Can't. Hurts. Help me."

"I will." Kayla drew figure eights over her stomach with the same unbreakable patience. The gesture soothed even as it inflamed. "You never have to lock this away again, Dev. You should have approached me. I would have given you what you needed."

Somehow Kay knew. Though she generally wallowed in the wild treatment of the crew, it would have shattered her today. Today, she needed calmness. Supple hands kneaded her knotted muscles. Kayla drew on her massage experience to blow Devon away.

When she added her lips to the steady manipulation of her magic fingers, Dev cried out. She arched, thrusting her hips at Kayla. Thankfully her friend didn't tease. She laid her mouth beside Devon's dripping flesh and blew a stream of cool, refreshing air over the puffy tissue.

If Kay had latched on to her steaming pussy directly, Devon would probably have rocketed through the roof. Kayla understood.

She took care of Devon. The lush fall of her midnight hair brushed softness across Dev's leg.

Open-mouthed kisses started on the tops of her thighs and circled closer to the entrance of her pussy. When Kayla lipped her mound, Devon's spine flexed, offering herself for whatever her friend chose to do to her.

In the background, a world away, Dave uttered a steady stream of encouragement to his wife. When Devon could tune in for more than the general buzz, she caught things like "yeah, you're driving her crazy" or "she's soaked, must taste delicious".

She hadn't realized she'd flung her hands out until Neil and James each claimed one. They twined their fingers with hers, lending her strength and enhancing her pleasure. With painstaking delicacy, Kayla extended her tongue toward Devon's pussy.

Everyone in the room held their breath.

Devon flexed her hips even as Kay descended. The moment they touched, both of them moaned. Kayla insinuated her wriggling muscle between Devon's saturated folds. She rimmed the opening of her pussy before lapping at the juices spilling freely from her core. Her nose nudged Devon's clit as she buried her face and ate as though she were seated at a five-star restaurant.

"Damn," Neil rasped. "She looks pretty fucking good at that."

"Agh!" Devon knew they'd interpret her unintelligible shout correctly.

"I want to learn how to do that flicky thing." Joe grunted from the couch. Devon looked up in time to see Morgan smack his hand when he reached for his own cock. She tormented him with a few more deep strokes on his erection before pulling off to observe.

"Can you see, Dev?" Neil released her hand to slide closer, propping her head on his ribs. "Watch how she makes each pass a work of art. She's relishing your taste. Her lips are so shiny. I bet she'd taste so good if you kissed her again."

The thought alone was enough to cause shockwaves to radiate from Devon's overripe clit. She clawed the feather bed, trying to hold on. It was no use.

"It's okay. Plenty more, remember?" Kayla's permission vibrated through Devon's pussy, ensuring her surrender. She came harder than she expected. Wetness gushed from her channel, released by the dam breaking inside her. Though her men had treated her to unlimited delights, something about having this woman provide her satisfaction dialed the intensity up.

Kayla hummed as she drank every drop of the lust and satisfaction she'd inspired. She shifted, while Devon still shuddered and quaked. Not to abandon Dev at the height of her pleasure, but to raise her higher instead. The taller woman used her long limbs to spread Devon's knees as far as possible. Dave held one while James accepted the other. The men kept her spread while Kayla latched on to her pussy once more.

Devon expected overstimulation to hurt, stealing some of her glow. It didn't. Kayla sucked softly, easing Dev back to their joining. She fanned the passion before it had a chance to dim very much.

"Neil, do the honors here, would you?" Dave jerked his chin toward Devon's knee. Her partner shuffled until he rested by her side. James and Neil held her while Dave crawled somewhere behind Kay, out of Devon's range of vision.

The glassy-smooth motion of Kayla's licking stuttered. She groaned against Devon's pussy.

"Dave is playing with her," James informed Devon with a strained whisper. "He's dipping his fingers in her pussy and sucking on her clit. I've never seen her so eager before."

Devon couldn't believe it when another orgasm rushed her system. From nowhere, the intense relief sideswiped her, leaving her completely defenseless. She'd fantasized about this for so long that being here, with the woman and men they loved, was enough to set her over the edge again and again.

This time Kay joined her, if the broken cries bouncing off her tender flesh were any indication. True to her word, Kay didn't fall to the mattress, replete. If anything, the flood of passion encouraged her to amplify their rapture. She crawled up Devon's body like a lioness on the prowl. Her tattoos danced and rippled with the sinuous flexing of her body.

Devon was surprised when the taste of her own slick come on Kayla's mouth inflicted another aftershock instead of mild distaste. She devoured their mingled flavor. Where their kisses might have been rough if it had been woman to man or harsh if man to man, even at the height of their passion, they elected to meet with intensity over force.

Kayla stared directly into her eyes as they kissed.

Dev wrapped her hands around Kay's lush waist. She tried to guide the larger woman where she preferred. Kayla beat her to it, already in motion. She scissored their legs so that one of her knees landed between Devon's and she straddled one of Devon's thighs.

Two could play this game.

Devon planted the sole of her foot on the mattress, raising her leg until Kayla couldn't help but ride the sleek pillar of her body. At first it was enough to grind their pussies on each other's legs, searing heat to cool skin. Their hips rotated as they rubbed themselves on their friend.

"Mother of God." Neil sounded as if he might pass out from excitement. "That's the sexiest thing I've ever seen."

Kayla slipped closer with each swing of her body over Devon until they'd knit as tight as could be. Slightly sideways, the position left Kayla rubbing her clit over Devon's mound. Another shift and they met, clit to clit.

Devon squealed and came again, each climax stretching into the next as her pleasure extended. Kayla glided above her, slipping against their joined, moist flesh. Devon knew she couldn't take much more before she overdosed on excitement. She lunged upward, latching on to Kayla's breast, sucking with enough force to transmit her sense of urgency.

Kay obeyed, convinced by the additional sensation. Their movements became choppy and desperate yet no less graceful. Kayla sat up straighter. She rode Devon, making sure to rub her pussy over as much of her delta as possible with each pass. When their stares collided, both women surrendered to the moment and the success of their experimental ardor.

They peaked together.

The release seemed to cascade in endless increments, lingering so long they rested in each other's arms. When Devon could open her eyes again, it was to a marvelous sight.

Dave, James and Neil attempted to match the passion their wives had generated. The three men locked together in a licentious chain that resembled a triple stack of Legos, each peg fasted to the hole in front of it. James in front, Dave in the middle, Neil behind them both. They fucked as if there was an award for most strokes per minute. Damn, Dave and James would be sore tomorrow.

A feminine cry from the couch drew Devon's attention. Morgan and Kate rode their guys. They'd opted for reverse cowgirl, seated so they faced out toward the group. A pair of naughty bookends. Four sets of eyes refused to blink as their owners joined in creating passion that radiated throughout the room.

Mike and Joe reached around their wives' waists to rub their clits or test the constricting rings of muscle hugging their cocks below. The guys thrust upward into their women with strokes so well timed they stayed in lockstep for as long as Devon could watch.

A strangled cry brought her attention back to the pile of men beside her and Kayla. She reached out to stroke James's cock, which bobbed and slapped his abdomen with every rough thrust from Dave. Each motion impaled James even as it withdrew Neil from Dave's ass. On the return journey, Dave shoved Neil deep in his own ass while granting James's prostate a moment of relief.

The cycle couldn't last forever. The men grunted and cursed as they fucked, already driven to the boundary of their restraint by the demonstration Kayla and Devon had given them.

"Oh, fuck." James didn't manage to give more warning than that before thick white strands shot from his erection. The first jet erupted with enough force to tag him in the chin. The purple head of his cock appeared even darker when pearly fluid streaked his olive skin. Blast after blast iced his pecs, abs and Devon's fingers.

He stared into her eyes as he surrendered, showing her how much he loved what he'd witnessed. All of her, as well as the men filling him. Dave jerked in Neil's hold, emptying himself in James's pulsing ass. Devon smiled. Guys never could resist the tug of his ring of muscles during orgasm. It yanked Neil with him every time.

The same was probably true for Dave. In a slutty domino fall, Neil caved while Dave's ass twitched and clamped around the long cock embedded in it. Neil fucked Dave, held his friend close, but never once did the big man's stare leave Kayla's face.

I love you, he mouthed to his wife as he shattered.

Kayla trembled in Devon's arms.

Dev rubbed the other woman's back, aware that they'd continued their subtle gyrations throughout the magnificent exchange their guys indulged in. As everyone turned to watch the two couples on the couch, they picked up the pace.

Devon moaned long and low when Kay added a swivel of her hips to every bump and grind. She'd thought they were through. It seemed they'd only rested. Passion flared again. She smacked Kayla's ass—whether to encourage or rebuke her, she didn't give a damn anymore.

They watched together as Mike and Joe rose from the couch without leaving their wives' bodies. They turned as one, lowering the women to their knees on the floor, bent over the seat of the couch they now faced. Kate looked toward Morgan and they both smiled as their husbands fucked them hard, fast and perfectly.

The best friends reached out, lacing their fingers on top of the center cushion.

As if they felt that connection, Joe and Mike growled in unison. Their knuckles turned white where they gripped their wives' asses. Buried to the hilt, they sprayed their semen as deep as possible into their women.

Devon sighed as she thought about how perfect it would be if both women conceived after today's session. Being a part of building their family seemed fitting. After all, they'd shared one of the most personal experiences of her life and enhanced it with their presence.

The two couples stretched out, Mike and Kate lying on the couch and Joe and Morgan snuggled on the floor in front of it. Both men cradled their wives, angled toward the mattress where her and Kayla had interlocked.

"Have one more in you?" Kay sipped at the light perspiration sheening the skin behind her ear. "Come on, Dev. I know you do."

They writhed together, their pussies rubbing against each other as if they'd done this a million times before. The jewelry in Kayla's hood nudged Devon's clit. Metal beads ran across her hypersensitive flesh. The bar linking the nodules pressed and rolled her engorged nub.

Devon gasped.

"Now you see why I like them so much. They're not just pretty. They're functional." Kayla gathered her breasts and used them to paint circles over Devon's chest. When they both needed more, Kay stretched to her full length, proffering one of the mounds to Devon.

Without altering the flowing motion of her hips, she fed her breast into Dev's gaping mouth. Devon couldn't stop herself from suckling the tight peak or playing with the hoop piercing the darker tissue there. Having something soft yet heavy in her mouth while Kay stroked every inch of her body calmed her, allowing her to focus on the ecstasy spiraling higher inside her once more, enhanced the sensations.

"Yeah." Kayla grunted, then slid her hand beneath Devon's head. Her friend clasped her close to her heart, granting no quarter, though Devon would never have asked for any. She mashed their pelvises together faster and faster, her ass shaking in the seductive motion shared by all rutting animals.

Devon surrendered to Kayla, allowed herself to be used as a warm body for Kay to slake her lust on. In the process, she gleaned plenty of pleasure for herself.

She tried to warn Kayla that she was losing control. The breast filling her mouth with sweet warmth prevented her from uttering anything intelligible.

Kay seemed to understand regardless. "Yes. Yes. Come with me, Devon. One more time."

Kayla froze, then resumed her humping double-time. She came on top of Devon, her pussy kissing Devon's with the force of her orgasm. Dev feared she might have lost the thread of her arousal in the wake of the awe of beholding such a tremendous release.

Until she felt the stroking of six masculine hands over her arms, legs and anywhere else James, Neil and Dave could reach. Someone tapped the sweet spot on her neck and she was a goner. She spasmed beneath Kayla's weight, nearly throwing the limp woman across the room with the force of her seizing.

Passion overwhelmed her, leaving her nerves ragged and exposed. She whimpered, thrashing and caught in the throes of rapture so strong it scared her. When she cried out, a reassuring kiss landed on her mouth.

James gathered her to him, pacifying her as every muscle in her body twitched then died. Boneless, she allowed him and Neil to sandwich her between them. Kayla pressed between Neil's back and Dave's front. Their fingers still linked, they drifted for quite some time.

Minutes or maybe hours later, Devon heard rustling from the direction of the couch. When she lifted her head to check out the situation, her gaze met Kayla's. Her friend smiled, a little timid, then nuzzled into her husband's arm. "Still alive?"

"I think so." Devon couldn't stop her blush. Could things be normal between them? What would change in the aftermath of their exchange? "Are we good?"

"You're fucking terrific." Mike grunted following a smack, likely Kate reprimanding his smartassery in such a critical moment.

Devon couldn't thank him enough. Both women exchanged a grin.

"You know, I think he's right." Devon beamed. "We *were* amazing. Thank you."

"Anytime. I loved every minute. It's so different. Soft, gentle... I'd almost forgotten how good it could be." Kay sighed. "I was so afraid you'd freak. Change your mind. After that, I couldn't handle it if you were grossed out or things got weird."

"Me either." Tears stung Devon's eyes. Damn, she'd done enough of that lately.

"If it fits, it can't be wrong." James rained Eskimo kisses on her nose.

"That's what *he* said," Kayla murmured. Being half-asleep didn't thwart her bad joke.

"Yes. Yes, I did." Dave made her giggle as he cuddled her close, both of them resting in the arms of their beloved mate after sharing their needs and granting the other permission to find what they could not provide personally.

Devon couldn't imagine a deeper expression of love than that.

Unless it was the serenity she felt when her guys bundled her between them, whispering how well she did, how sexy she was and how much they adored her. Now and always.

Nothing she could say could communicate the love exploding from her heart.

"It's okay, baby." Neil kissed her temple. "We know. Same goes."

"Ditto." James laid his head on her shoulder and closed his eyes. "Love you. Even if you are going to give me a fucking heart attack if you keep getting me that worked up."

"I love you, too." She sighed into the dusk falling over their shared space. "All of you."

And much later, when they snacked on leftovers of the decadent birthday cake Morgan had slaved over, Mike didn't wince. Not even when he devoured the thickest section of the frosting.

EPILOGUE

Two and a half weeks later, Kate emerged from the bathroom of her renovated home with Mike so close he might be glued to her backside. She rubbed one hand in a circle low on her belly and grinned. It was the sort of shit-eating variety reserved for winning the lotto or telling someone you've just gotten engaged. Or...

Morgan perked up, wondering if she had it right. The rest of the crew had assumed the pair was in the powder room for a quickie, but she had a feeling...

Besides, they'd been *far* too quiet for that.

Everyone held their breath.

"I'm pregnant."

No one noticed the tight smile Morgan and Joe exchanged. If they caught the tears falling from the corner of her eyes, they would assume they were manufactured by joy, not sadness. Because she hadn't shared the news they'd received when their tests had come back from the doctor yesterday. Hadn't quite finished processing it really.

Joe was sterile.

No baby grew in her womb, and it never would. Unless...

She couldn't dare to think such things when her friends celebrated one of the most magnificent events of their life. She'd have time to grieve later. Until then, she'd be the best aunt this child could hope for and take comfort in her friends' bliss.

It wouldn't be all sunshine and roses. She'd help them every step of the way, as they would have done for her if the situation had been reversed. Her own upbringing had taught her that a family is what you make it, not what you're given genetically.

The crew was a perfect example of that.

Joe's hand shook when it landed on her waist. She smiled up at him, hoping to erase some of the tight crinkles around his eyes. He suffered too. Maybe more than her. She'd promised him it didn't change anything between them. She loved him as much today as yesterday, more as each day grew the miraculous bond between them.

Still, after hugging Kate and taking his turn at offering felicitations, he stumbled from the room.

"What's wrong with Joe?" Kate paused, searching Morgan's eyes for signs of trouble. If she wasn't careful, her best friend would ferret out the drama and have them swaddled in her mothering before they'd properly celebrated her revelation.

"He's not feeling well. Probably doesn't want to risk getting you sick." She squeezed Kate's hand, hating herself for the lie. "I'd better go check on him."

"Okay." Kate chewed her lip. "Let me know if there's anything you need. Either of you."

"We will." Morgan smiled without a hint of pretense. "You're going to be the best mom in the history of the universe. I can't wait to spoil him or her."

"Him." Mike's arms folded across his chest. "I wouldn't know what the hell to do with a daughter. She'd be all gorgeous like her mom and I'd have to lock her up until she was seventy to keep boys from corrupting her."

"Oh, I can just see it now." Morgan patted the foreman on his puffed-up chest. "You're in so much trouble. A daughter it is."

"Shush." His face blanched a bit. "I could handle one little girl with my hands tied behind my back, right?"

"That's what *he* said," Kayla sing-songed. The eight friends cramped in the kitchen erupted into laughter at the horror in Mike's wide eyes. The raucous cheering still echoed in Morgan's ears as she burst from the house in search of her husband.

They would get through this. As long as they stuck together.

She scanned the deck and found it empty, so she jogged down the stairs and around the corner to the backyard. Joe leaned against a tree, his hands jammed in his pockets, head hanging, breathing hard.

Her heart broke all over again.

She slowed as she approached. As always, he knew when she was near. "Sorry. Just needed a minute."

Morgan threaded her hands between his bent elbows and his sides. She splayed one hand low on his flat abdomen and the other over his chest, infusing him with as much warmth as she could impart in the chilly afternoon air.

For a while they rested there together. She counted the beats of his heart as it slowed from pounding beneath her hand to a moderate thump. Eyes closed, she could have stayed there with him forever. Long before she was ready to let go, he roused, shifting in her hold.

He pivoted on his boot heel, turning to face her.

"That was really selfish. Shit." He scrubbed his hand through his hair, making it stick up in adorable disarray. She wondered if he'd remembered to make an appointment to get it cut.

"I don't think so." She reached up to cup his cheek. He leaned into her caress, heaving a sigh of relief or self-deprecation, she couldn't quite tell. "You're allowed to grieve. But don't shut me out. We're in this together, right?"

"Sorry for your luck." A rare fury entered his eyes, no doubt directed at himself.

Morgan had never had the urge to smack someone before. She yanked her hand away as if singed and took a hasty step back. She stumbled over a root from the gnarled old oak and would have fallen on her ass if he hadn't snagged her out of midair.

He buried his face in her hair, which she'd worn loose today just for him, and breathed deep. In the bakery, she always kept it in a bun. "I'm fucking this all to hell and back."

She separated them enough to grin long and slow. "Come on. You know you want to say it."

"No, I don't." How did he manage to be so fucking cute even when he pouted?

She chucked his chin. "Sure, you do. It's pretty fun once you get the hang of it."

"Fine. That's what *he* said." A ghost of a smile touched his extra-fine lips.

She couldn't help but smother it in a kiss until it blossomed into his radiant grin. "I love you, Joe. There are other ways. We can adopt. Something. Maybe being an aunt and uncle will be enough."

His grimace called her bluff.

The back door banged open hard enough to be a warning.

"Hey, are you all right, Joe?" Dave clomped along the deck, giving them plenty of heads up as he approached.

"Yeah," Joe called. He hugged Morgan. "I will be."

"In that case, the girls are pitching a fit because you booked it before they could unveil their big deal." Dave probably rolled his eyes. "You're going to have to be on your deathbed, or hurling at least, if you don't get your ass inside soon."

"I promise you'll enjoy this." Morgan stroked his cheek, surreptitiously swiping the lingering moisture at the corner of his eye before his crewmate could spot it. She hated keeping secrets, but this wasn't the right time to share their disappointment. "It's not very often that *I* get to surprise *you*."

"I don't deserve you." He dropped his head to her shoulder.

She would have ripped him a new one, then smothered him in affection until he couldn't deny the breadth of her love except Dave rounded the corner of the deck just then, spotting them.

"You sure everything's cool?" The big man chewed his lip.

"I love you." Morgan rubbed as much of his back as she could reach in their embrace.

"That's everything to me," Joe whispered in her ear. "We can survive anything as long as we have each other, right?"

"Right." She squeezed him tight.

"I'm sure." Joe enveloped her hand in his, then headed toward his friend. "We will be okay."

"If there's anything I can do…" Dave lost his jovial mask.

"Not right now." Joe shook his head.

Morgan's eyes burned when Dave hugged Joe and her husband didn't resist.

Then, as if by some Jedi mind trick, the two men snapped into their usual routine. "Probably have some pussy hangnail, is that it?"

"Yeah, just like that time you cried over the splinter." Joe socked Dave in his biceps. His loose fist bounced off a wall of muscle.

"Dude. That was a four-inch sliver of wood, and it went *through* my fucking hand."

Morgan had wondered how he'd earned the jagged scar. The crew had plenty of those.

"Flesh wound." Joe snugged Morgan tight to his torso as they climbed the deck stairs.

She wrapped her arm around his waist and rested her head near his heart. When they reentered the space, the whole crew looked up. Dave gave his head a barely discernible shake, so they all went about their business.

"Okay, ready?" Devon practically bounced next to a flat rectangle covered by a sheet.

Morgan took her place next to a similar package, the only one left that didn't have one of her best friends standing nearby. She fisted her hands in the soft, worn material draping it and winked up at Joe.

"We realize we're a day early, but since we all have plans tomorrow, we wanted to give you your gifts today. Together. Happy Valentine's Day," Kate said to Mike. The rest of them echoed the sentiment.

"One…two…"

They whipped the covers off the framed photos simultaneously.

Someone whistled, maybe James.

"Whoa." Joe crouched in front of the artwork. He trailed his finger over the likeness of her, reverence in every brush of his fingertip.

"I think I'm having a heart attack." Dave clutched his chest. "Please tell me you kept this outfit."

"I'll show you tomorrow." Kayla smirked.

The guys rushed to their wives, showing them exactly how much they loved their gifts—so much more than the physical presents the women had schemed to concoct. Mike swung Kate into his arms and twirled her around the kitchen while his best friends paired, or trebled, off to indulge in some one-on-one, or   -two, affection.

"You know, our evil plot was to use these to take you as our horny hostages and issue tons of naughty demands..." Kate shrugged. "But you've already given us everything we wished for and more."

Mike pried his stare away from the likeness of his wife in her sexy lace catsuit long enough to glance over his shoulder at the rest of the crew and nod. He cleared his throat. "That's what *we* said."

WHAT HAPPENS TO THE CREW NEXT? KEEP READING TO FIND OUT!

HAMMER IT HOME

POWERTOOLS

JAYNE RYLON

When times get tough, the tough stage one scorching-hot intervention.

Morgan is happy that her best friend Kate is expecting the crew's littlest member, but helping renovate a room for a nursery is more than she can bear. Baby furniture and pastel paint are a painful reminder that she and Joe can't—and will never—conceive. There's no hiding it from the rest of the close-knit crew, either.

True to their unique brand of love, the gang rallies to find a non-traditional solution to alleviate their friends' suffering. Not with a cold, clinical visit to a sperm donation clinic, but delivering it the old-fashioned way. With a healthy dose of searing passion.

But soon after Morgan's scorching hot night with her husband's four best friends, an accident threatens the life of one of those men. The challenges that lie ahead will test the crew's powerful bond to the limit—and their long-standing promise to take care of each other through good, bad, and sexy times. Whatever it takes...

Warning: Not everything in life turns out as planned, but with love all odds are surmountable. Especially when those odds include five hot construction workers on your side. Contains m/m/f group ménage scenes.

EXCERPT FROM HAMMER IT HOME, POWERTOOLS BOOK 6

She expected Joe to take the fork to the right, which led to the private cabin where their friends lived and most of the crew's interludes took place. Instead, he veered left. Toward the cute bungalows the crew had recently expanded on in response to the initial success of Kay's venture.

Several of them hadn't even opened to guests yet.

Morgan didn't ask where they were going. She trusted Joe to take her where she needed to be. As long as he was by her side, it didn't much matter where they ended up. Good thing her faith in him thrived. The truck slowed in the middle of nowhere until they rolled to a stop in the center of the rustic road.

When he removed a strip of black silk from his back pocket, she knew what she expected. Her lashes rested against her cheeks as she closed her eyes, leaning toward her husband.

"Sweet girl." He fastened the fabric around her head tight enough that she couldn't peek even if she'd tried to open her eyes, yet loose enough to be comfortable.

"For now." The hint of naughty she added to her response had the desired effect.

Joe's voice turned husky. "I like you spicy too."

The anticipated kiss she craved never arrived. The truck started off down the road. She threw her hand out, searching for the handle on the door or the edge of the seat. Joe's fingers landed high on her thigh. "I've got you."

"I know."

"Almost there." He crooned to her in soft, steady murmurs, never letting her forget he sat by her side. "I see lights now. And there's the crew. They're waiting for you."

"For us."

"True, for us." After a quick squeeze, his hand abandoned her leg long enough to unfasten her seatbelt. "Go with Dave. I'm right behind you."

Before she could respond, the truck door opened. Huge hands engulfed her waist. She floated into their grasp. "You look really nice tonight, Morgan."

Thank goodness she hadn't worn a dress with a short skirt or she'd be flashing her butt to the entire forest. Not that the eight people she couldn't see but knew were there hadn't gotten an eyeful of every inch of her already.

Soon they'd be doing a whole lot more than looking too.

Dave's boots thudded on what sounded like wooden treads as they ascended together. The new buildings had adorable porches complete with swings. That must be where they were. She hadn't observed the progress personally, though Joe had told her the crew had decided to take a couple weeks off before starting their next project to help Kay out.

Someone cursed softly. A subtle creak made her sure they'd opened a door for her and Dave. "So sexy, Morgan."

"Thank you, James."

"I'm going to set you down." Dave murmured to her as he lowered her feet to the floor. He braced her shoulders. Scuffles and whispers surrounded her as her friends all assembled as they saw fit. "Joe's got you now."

The big man's hand swapped out for her husband's familiar grasp. Dotted kisses at her temple had her sighing while he worked the knot on her blindfold loose. A steady white noise piqued her curiosity. What could that be? "Tonight is special. For all of us. We wanted you to know how much. Live in the moment, Mo. Take what we're giving."

He whipped the silk from her, letting it slither to the floor unnoticed.

Blinking against the sudden light, she tried to focus. When she did, a sheen of tears immediately turned the flickering candles into glittering sparkles, dazzling her. She reached out. Joe held one hand while Dave collected the other.

"You did all this for me?" The whisper cut through the hush of her eight best friends, who awaited her reaction. Behind the naked, oiled men who stood shoulder to shoulder and their wives—adorned in gossamer togas that hid the bare essentials, proclaiming their intent to sit the festivities out—sheer panels of iridescent fabric draped from exposed wooden rafters.

Zillions of tiny clear lights, like the ones hugging their tree at Christmas, hung behind the soft falls. She felt as though she'd taken up residence in an enchanted snow globe, or maybe a cloud way, way out in some ethereal paradise on the edge of the universe. Romance blossomed in every nook and cranny of the space. Pale silk flowers, warm vanilla candles on wrought-iron stands and the largest canopied bed she'd ever seen were just a few of the details bombarding her senses.

"We did it for both you and Joe." Kate smiled from her post with a fluffy white towel draped over her forearm. What the heck?

The guys stepped aside, chiseled bodies parting like a fleshy curtain at a beefcake ballet. Behind them, a waterfall trickled from what could have been a loft. A rivulet bounced next to vines that looked as real as the ones Kayla had cultivated in the gardens outside. Maybe they were.

Splashes drew her eye from expertly crafted faux stone to faux stone until droplets rained into an elaborate whirlpool fashioned from river rock on the outside and something natural yet smooth-looking in the basin. A gradual slope led up to the dais supporting the magical indoor pond. Lush greenery surrounded the pool. She suspected the window on the other side would grant glorious views of the lake if it were daytime.

A fireplace made from the same cut stone chased away any chill emanating from the glass.

"Whoa." Nothing more elaborate formed in her mind.

Awestruck, she allowed Joe to manipulate her, stripping her sweater over her head and freeing her from her lacey bra before she'd recovered. Next he slid her skirt from her hips, then lifted her from the puddle of gorgeous fabric. He swiped her shoes from her feet and patted her bare butt. No need to remove underwear. She hadn't bothered with panties.

"Nice touch, Mo."

She grinned over her shoulder at her husband. "Glad you approve."

"Now run along and play." A gentle shove inspired her to put one foot in front of the other, heading in the direction of the crew.

ABOUT THE AUTHOR

Jayne Rylon is a *New York Times* and *USA Today* bestselling author. She received the 2011 RomanticTimes Reviewers' Choice Award for Best Indie Erotic Romance.

Her stories used to begin as daydreams in seemingly endless business meetings, but now she is a full-time author, who employs the skills she learned from her straight-laced corporate existence in the business of writing. She lives in Ohio with two cats and her husband, the infamous Mr. Rylon.

When she can escape her purple office, Jayne loves to travel the world, SCUBA dive, take pictures, avoid speeding tickets in her beloved Sky and—of course—read.

Made in the USA
Las Vegas, NV
06 May 2022